SHANGHAIED!

by

ARTHUR CATHERALL

THE CHILDREN'S PRESS
LONDON AND GLASGOW

This Impression 1968

CONTENTS

CHAPTER ONE

LEFT ABOARD

AT ANCHOR in the river, a line of salt-encrusted trawlers waited for high water when they would be able to enter the fish dock and begin discharging their catch. They had come from as far north as Bear Island, from the bitter weather of the Murmansk coast, and from the Icelandic grounds. Some had been out for three weeks, others for a month. Their fish holds were crammed with prime cod, some of the catches being worth up to four thousand pounds, or more.

In the Fish Dock itself seven trawlers were waiting to start for the fishing grounds, and for the past twenty minutes members of the various crews had been hurrying along the docks, carrying their gear; black kitbags, oilskins, seaboots. These men wore no uniform, but there was no mistaking them for anything but deep-water men. They had the rolling gait which comes to all who man the ships which go "down north" in search of cod.

There was an unexpected and unusual visitor to the docks that morning, for a Rolls-Royce, its mellow horn sounding now and then, was driven carefully past large, rusting anchors, piles of old anchor chains, coils of new rope, and drums of lubricating oil. There were other drums which smelled strongly of cod livers, and over all was the odour of Stockholm tar.

The Rolls-Royce was brought to a stop alongside the three-hundred-ton trawler *Blackball Annie*, and a uniformed chauffeur sprang out smartly to open the door for an old man. Behind the old man came a youth of sixteen or seventeen years, and they were in striking contrast.

The old man was just over six feet, and though he must have passed his seventieth year, he carried himself erect and gave the impression of great strength. His shoulders were as square as those of many a man half his years. The youth was about five feet six, slim, and very smartly dressed in well-cut sports jacket, flannels, a canary yellow pullover, and light sports shoes. His flaxen hair was cut in the latest style, long and brushed back along the sides.

While the chauffeur was getting back into the driving seat, the old man turned to his grandson and said:

"Well, there you are, Harold, that's the *Annie*; one of the finest trawlers afloat. I sailed in her when she was new from the shipbuilders, and I worked my way up to being her skipper. She was the first trawler I bought. I love her. She's tough, just as I was when I sailed in her."

Harold Jackson smiled and nodded, but made no comment. The smile suggested that he had heard all this before. Then, as his grandfather made for the single plank which acted as gangway for the *Blackball Annie*, Harold turned for a moment to speak to the chauffeur.

"Jenkins, don't forget, when we're going home I want to call at the Sports Outfitters for a new tennis racquet. Remind me if I forget."

"Yes, sir," the chauffeur touched his peaked cap respectfully, and Harold turned to follow his grandfather aboard.

"Now, you have a look round . . . examine the engines," Josh Jackson suggested. "I want a word with Mike Grory, the skipper. I hope you'll meet him afterwards. One of the finest skippers we have . . . and reckoned to be the toughest nut that ever sailed out of these docks. Nearly as tough as I was, I reckon," and Josh smiled at some memory.

Harold nodded, then turned dutifully towards the stern, and the engine-room. He was bored, but his grandfather had been pestering him for a long time to visit the docks and see the trawlers which would one day belong to him, and as he was on long vacation, he had no excuse now. He consoled himself with the thought that it must be nearly high tide, which meant the trawlers would sail, and then they could get away for lunch. He was playing tennis that afternoon.

While he clambered carefully down into the heat and oily smell of the engine-room, old Josh was shaking hands with Mike Grory. Mike looked tough. He was tall, square built, and with a blue-black beard which made him look as if he was always in need of a shave.

"I thought you'd changed your mind and weren't coming, Mr. Jackson," Mike said, as he took the cigar old Josh offered him.

"Take another," Josh suggested. "I know you like a good cigar, and I want to put you in a good temper. I've got an awkward job for you."

"Well, I'll not light one now," Mike said, "we'll be sailing in a few minutes, and I like to smoke a cigar in peace."

"You'd better light the cigar now," old Josh advised, his eyes twinkling, "I'm going to destroy your peace. I came late because I've brought you an unwilling passenger."

"A what?" Mike paused in the act of cutting the end of his cigar.

"My grandson is knocking about somewhere, and though

he doesn't know it yet, he's going with you to Iceland . . . as a member of your crew."

Mike stared for a moment, then sucked busily at his cigar. Finally, throwing the spent match through the wheelhouse window he asked:

"Am I slowing-up in my old age, Mr. Jackson? You say he is coming with me, as a member of the crew . . . but he's coming unwillingly. Isn't that going to be a bit awkward?"

Josh grinned.

"It's going to be awkward for him, Mike. Now listen carefully. His father died on one of the Mediterranean convoys during the war. His mother was killed in an air raid." Josh spread his big hands in a gesture. "Therefore . . . he's an orphan. My wife and I brought him up . . . and my wife has spoiled him. The only grandchild we have, you see."

Mike nodded.

"Mind you, there's nothing really wrong with the lad," Josh went on. "He's smart enough; a good sportsman, does well in athletics, and so on . . . but he's grown up to think that the world was kind of made just for him. Always had everything he wants . . . clothes, money, holidays, everything."

"I see," Mike nodded to show his understanding. "That isn't good for anybody."

"I've brought him aboard the *Annie*," Josh went on, "to complete his education. One day he'll own this ship, Mike . . . he'll have everything I possess. He'll be managing director of the Jackson Trawlers, and I intend him to know just what it's like to go down north and trawl for fish."

"And that's a very good idea," Mike agreed, nodding his appreciation. "I always said you were as successful as you have been because you'd done all the trawling jobs yourself when you were younger."

"Well, Harold's going to do them . . . that's his name, Harold Jackson," Josh said, and now he was more sober. "I want him to be locked away somewhere until you've got down river. You're to treat him as a stowaway. Make him work . . . make him work hard, make him work at everything, stoking, potato-peeling, fish-gutting, icing, everything. He's got to see that the money he spends is earned by sweat and blood."

"Yes . . . yes," Mike said slowly, his eyes screwed-up a little as he thought deeply. Then, "Look, what do I say when he points out that he's your grandson?"

The twinkle came back into the old man's eyes.

"You just ask him to prove it," Josh said, chuckling. "I took the precaution of taking his wallet from his pocket before we left home. I've got it here," and he patted his own pocket. "He won't be able to prove a thing. I've thought this out, Mike. You have a word with the Ship's Runner, and get him to take Harold into the fish hold . . . and leave him there. You can let him out when you're well down river. Oh . . . one thing, make sure he doesn't dive overboard while you're in the river. He's a very good swimmer."

Mike called to the Ship's Runner, a shabby individual who was leaning against the rail, sucking a pencil stub. It was his job to ensure that no trawler went to sea without a full crew. If a deckhand failed to turn up, then the Ship's Runner would race off to get hold of some unemployed trawlerman who would be willing to sign on at a moment's notice.

"There's a young fellow aboard, Joe, probably in the

engine-room," Mike said quietly, "I want you to get hold of him and show him round the fish hold. Take him in there, leave him in, and put the hatch cover in place. Do it as quickly and as quietly as possible . . . and then forget it."

Joe stared for a moment, then grinned. Mike gave him half a crown as he turned back to the wheelhouse. Joe knew all the members of the crew, so asked no questions.

Back in the wheelhouse Mike assured Josh that the plan had been begun. Harold was to be locked in the fish hold.

"That'll cool his heels a bit," Josh agreed. "Treat him rough. I want the conceit knocked out of him."

"You can leave that to me," Mike assured him, smiling.

"You might have your hands full," Josh warned him. "He takes after me in some ways. He's got a will of his own."

"I'll break him," Mike said quietly.

They stood talking for a few minutes until a shout went up:

"Baskets are up!"

On either side of the lock which enabled ships to go from dock to river, and *vice versa*, were two short masts. In daytime two yellow baskets were hoisted when the tide was at full and the lock gates open. At night two green lights were the signal. Now the baskets were up.

Josh went ashore after shaking hands with Mike and wishing him a successful voyage. The uniformed chauffeur looked rather startled when Harold did not appear.

"He's decided to take a trip to Iceland, Jenkins," Josh said, his eyes twinkling, "and that's the story you'll tell my wife if she asks. You understand?"

"Er . . . yes, sir; very good, sir," Jenkins replied. "There's the question of a tennis racquet. Mr. Harold said we were to call at the Sports Outfitters and . . ."

"He won't be thinking of tennis for at least three weeks," Josh assured him. "Now . . . off we go. Harold is taking a course in deep-sea trawling. I'm sure he'll look back on it with pleasure . . . a few years hence."

He knocked the ash from his cigar and settled back in his seat, while aboard the *Blackball Annie* the Ship's Runner had just called up to Mike Grory in the wheelhouse:

"Everything's hunky-dory, Mr. Grory. I pretended I dropped the candle in the fish hold, and then I scrammed. I dropped the hatch cover in place and put the wedges in. He'll not get out in a hurry."

"Thanks, and . . . forget it, Joe. Understand, forget it. Nobody else knows?"

"The lad knows; I know, and you know," the Ship's Runner chuckled, then vaulted easily over the rail and on to the dockside. He waved a farewell to the wheelhouse as Skipper Mike Grory moved the engine-room telegraph pointer from "Stand by engines" to "Slow astern". The aft mooring ropes were cast off, and, as water boiled under the trawler's stern, the little vessel began to ease gently away from the dockside. The bow moorings were cast off, more bells rang in the engine-room, water boiled under the stern, and after a few seconds the *Blackball Annie* eased gently forward to take her place in the queue of trawlers waiting to pass through the lock pit and into the river. In a few minutes the trip to Iceland would have really begun.

CHAPTER TWO

THE "STOWAWAY" DISCOVERED

A DECKHAND had come to take the wheel, and a third person also entered the wheelhouse, the latter was Mat Webber, mate of the trawler. Mat was six inches shorter than the skipper, and built like a barrel. His face was the colour of mahogany, and might have been chipped from granite. He had that rugged look which suggests great strength. He nodded to Mike Grory, then began to roll a cigarette.

While waiting for the trawlers ahead to negotiate the lock-pit Mike took his mate on one side, and in a whisper informed him:

"We've got a stowaway under the hatches, Mat. No, listen," he warned, as Mat Webber stiffened indignantly. "We don't throw him ashore. He's a special kind of stowaway. We've got to handle him a bit rougher than an ordinary stowaway. I'll tip you off later on how to treat him. I'm just warning you now in case he should appear. *He's not to be put ashore.*"

Mat raised his bushy eyebrows, but made no comment. The trawlers ahead were moving, and once again bells jangled in the bowels of the *Annie*, and the deckboards vibrated as the engines were opened up a little.

There were a number of people on the sides of the lock, wives, mothers and sweethearts of the deckhands, come to wave goodbye to their menfolk, for trawling is a risky business, and no one can tell when a trawler goes out whether she will ever return. The gales and the icy seas of the sub-Arctic claim victims every year. Men are washed overboard, and are never seen again. Good ships go aground and are pounded to a tangle of battered plates in a few hours, or vanish without a trace.

Mike Grory waved to his wife, and then turned his attention once more to the navigation. In a few minutes they were out in the river, and the engine-room telegraph went over to "Full speed ahead". The water in the river was yellow with mud and sand. There were twin lines of dancing buoys to mark the fairway, but in an hour or so they would be in the open sea. Short of an accident, they would not return for three weeks, and in that time Harold Jackson, grandson of old Josh, was to be given a taste of the rougher side of trawling.

Mike gave Mat Webber a whispered explanation concerning the stowaway, speaking very quietly so that the deckhand at the wheel would hear nothing. There were to be only two people aboard who would know the identity of the, as yet unsuspected, stowaway.

Mat's eyes opened wide as he learned about Harold. Then he grinned and flipped the stub of his cigarette out through the wheelhouse window.

"Well, all I can say, Mike, is that old Josh is a good picker. He couldn't have put his grandson aboard a better trawler. If he wants this spoiled kid to see the rough side of it . . . well, I think we can do the job. Yes . . . I'm going to enjoy this."

Mike nodded, but said nothing, and for the next twenty minutes the *Annie* ploughed down river at eight knots. Then a deckhand, who had come up from the fo'c'sle paused, turned to stare towards the fish hatch coaming, and after going across to listen, hurried to the wheelhouse. Standing by the big winches which are situated on deck in front of the wheelhouse, he shouted:

"I think we've got a stowaway aboard, skipper. There's somebody in the hold, banging away like mad and shouting to be let out."

"You're drunk," Mat Webber shouted, and slammed the wheelhouse window shut again.

For a moment the deckhand stood staring up at the closed window, his face a mask of anger, then he turned and walked for'ard again. By this time, however, the third hand was on deck and he, too, had heard the banging on the fish hold hatch cover. He stood for a moment, listening, then began to kick away the wooden wedges which held the cover in position.

"Mate swore I was drunk," the deckhand said bitterly as he joined the third hand.

"Well, we're both drunk if there isn't anybody down there," was the laughing retort, and the third hand kicked away the last wedge. "We'll soon see, anyway. Oops, here they come."

The moment the last wedge was kicked free the hatch cover was thrown violently upwards, revealing Harold, standing on the ladder beneath. His face was pale, and blue from cold, and his eyes were blazing with anger.

Scrambling up on deck, he stood for a moment trying to stop the chattering of his teeth. The fish hold was half filled with many tons of ice, to be used later to keep the catch of cod as fresh as possible. It was cold down there, far too cold for anyone clad as Harold was. His sports vest, thin silk shirt, yellow pullover and light sports jacket, had been poor defence against the biting cold. There were goose-pimples up his arms, his neck and his cheeks.

"Where's the crazy fool who fastened me in there?" Harold demanded, finally conquering his chattering teeth. "The silly clot dropped his candle, and then went off. By the time I got to the ladder the hatch had been put on. Are you all deaf? I've been banging on the hatch for hours."

The deckhand and the third hand listened in silence. Then they both began to laugh. Harold did look rather funny. His face had a bluish tinge from the cold, but he must somehow have got dirt on one of his hands, wiped it across his face, and now he had a perfect imitation of a black moustache across his cheeks and upper lip.

Harold was not accustomed to people laughing at him, and if he had been angry before, he now became almost livid with fury.

"What are you laughing at you . . . you clots? Where's my grandfather? I'll have you kicked off the ship at once. Where is he? Where's my grandfather?"

That did stop the laughter, but only for a moment. Then the third hand turned to the man at his side and said:

"Here, George, I saw you putting something in your pocket. Give the lad his grandfather . . . come on, before he starts blubbing."

They both began to laugh again, and Harold made to push past them. The third hand blocked the way, and Harold pushed out a hand to sweep the man aside. Unfortunately, at that moment, the *Annie* gave a little lurch as the wheel was put over to change course. The hand which should have taken the third hand in the chest now took him in the face, and it certainly stopped him from laughing. The smack was so unexpected that the third hand staggered back, and catching his heel against a ring bolt in the deck he staggered and sat down heavily in the scuppers.

The deckhand stared owlishly, as if waiting for the skies to fall on this youth. The third hand was not the kind of man to put up with that sort of treatment, certainly not without doing something drastic in return.

Harold was striding towards the wheelhouse when the third hand scrambled to his feet. Now there was no silence, for the fall in the scuppers had hurt the third hand, physically, and in his dignity. His language was blue, and his threats ought to have made Harold's hair stand on end.

What would have happened if Mat Webber had not come down from the wheelhouse will never be known, for the third hand was strong, an ex-boxer, and in a very bad temper. Luckily for Harold, the mate was on deck in time to stop the massacre which might have followed.

Realising that he had lost his chance, the third hand stood and listened as Mat Webber roared:

"Where in tarnation d'you reckon you've come from, and what are you doing here? Hey? Answer. Don't stand there like a month-dead codfish."

It was not the spate of questions which stopped Harold in his tracks, it was the mate's voice. Mat Webber was proud of his voice, and fond of boasting that his tonsils were of brass and his throat copper-lined. He had the kind of voice which sergeant-majors use on a crowded parade ground. It was a voice which could be heard above the scream and fury of an Arctic gale, and it made Harold's hair stand on end.

"Well," Mat went on, his eyes blazing, his brown face thrust so close that Harold had to retreat a pace. "Answer me! Haven't you got a tongue in your head? You're a stowaway, that's what you are, you yard-and-a-half of bilge water; and I'll show you what we do with your sort."

Mat would not have made such a scene with an ordinary stowaway, but he felt that if Josh Jackson's grandson was to be tamed, then it was best to start in the toughest way possible. Grabbing Harold by the coat front, he gave him a shake which ought to have rattled every tooth in his head.

It was that indignity which brought Harold to life. No one had ever done anything like that to him before. For as long as he could remember people had been polite to him; back at the big house there were servants to answer every command. He had only to press a bell-push to have someone asking what he desired. To be yelled at by this brown-faced thug, and to be shaken like a bundle of rags frayed Harold's temper to breaking point. He reacted at once, hitting out as hard as he could.

His fist took Mat Webber flush on the nose, and if the mate of the *Annie* was tough, that punch was also tough. It's aim was right, and the timing was right. Tears filled Mat's eyes as if a tap had been turned on, and the shock was such that he immediately released his grip on Harold's coat.

For a few seconds there was an awed silence. One or two deckhands had come up from the fo'c'sle to find out what the shouting was about. They stood with the third hand, gaping at this indignity. Not one of them had ever seen Mat Webber punched on the nose in this fashion, especially by a stripling such as Harold.

Mat lifted his hand, wiped his nose with the knuckle part, and then gave a howl of fury.

A herring gull on top of the wheelhouse spread its wings and flew away, startled by the yell. Harold Jackson stepped back a pace, lifting his hands to defend himself; but the battle royal never started. A window in the wheelhouse was pushed open and Mike Grory yelled:

"Mr. Webber!"

The two curt words saved Harold from a punch which might have altered the shape of his face, for the mate of the *Annie* had fists like iron, and he knew how to use them. At the shout he checked, and turned. Then, to Harold he said icily:

"I'll remember that, m'lad. There isn't a fellow breathing from Reykjavik to Gibraltar ever clouted me across the nose an' got away with it. Now . . . get up to the wheelhouse before I forget myself, and pulverise you."

Quivering inwardly though he was, Harold had not forgotten he was the grandson of Josh Jackson, owner of the *Annie*, and in an equally icy voice he said:

"I won't forget what you did to me, either. When you get ashore I'd advise you to start looking for a fresh ship . . . and not aboard a Jackson trawler. You won't work on this ship again; I'll assure you of that."

Then, while Mat stood and choked back a flow of salty sea language which would have turned the air blue, Harold marched towards the ladder leading to the wheelhouse. Mat followed a yard to the rear, and to add insult to injury, the moment Harold was in the wheelhouse he slammed the door shut, just as the mate was about to enter. The door struck him solidly, and almost sent him down to the deck below.

Facing Mike Grory Harold said curtly:

"Am I to understand you are captain of this ship?"

Mike had been leaning on the ledge which ran round the wheelhouse, and he raised himself to stare at the pale-faced Harold. After a moment he said quietly:

"I don't know what you understand, young man. From the looks of you I don't suppose you understand very much. You look the sort of brainless young idiot I never like to meet."

He paused and knocked the ash off the cigar he was smoking, while Harold flinched and went even paler. Then, before he could think of anything cutting to say, Mike Grory went on: "Anyway, brainless or not, what are you doing aboard my ship? Do you know it's a criminal offence to stow away? There isn't room aboard a trawler for addle-headed young fools like you. When we get back to port you'll face the Magistrates . . . and I hope they fine you heavily."

"When we get back to port!" Harold laughed, a bitter scornful laugh. Then, and there was a sneer in his voice, he continued: "You listen to me, and I'll trouble you to be more polite when you address me. I happen to be Mr. Harold Jackson, grandson of the owner of this trawler," and with that he leaned against the side of the wheelhouse and waited for the look of embarrassment he hoped to see steal over Mike Grory's face. He was certain there would be apologies, and suggestions as to how soon he could be put ashore.

Mike Grory puffed at his cigar, while from the doorway Mat Webber grunted, a sarcastic grunt which made Harold flush.

"That's an original idea," Mike Grory finally admitted. "I've never heard anyone try that yarn before. The only trouble is I know it isn't true." Then, and his voice suddenly becoming fierce, he snapped: "Why, you little fool, what sort of a man do you think I am to swallow a yarn like that? You're not talking to one of your street-corner pals now. What are you doing aboard my ship? Been trying to steal something, I suppose, and got locked below, eh? Not quick enough for once. I've seen your kind before. Cheap little thieves, that's what your sort are."

"Thief! THIEF!" Harold choked over the word. "Why . . . why, you blithering idiot . . . oh . . . you wait until my grandfather hears what kind of men he has running his trawlers, he'll . . ."

"Take him away, Mr. Mate," Mike said coldly, and turned to stare through the window at the river ahead.

"Come on, m'lad," Mat said, laying a heavy hand on Harold's arm. "I'll put you where you'll cool off a bit."

"Take your filthy paws off me," Harold shouted, and breaking free he shouted at Mike: "You send me out of here if you dare. I'll soon show you who I am. I've got proof of my identity in my pocket, and . . ." his voice faltered, and a look of uncertainty spread over his face.

"Well," Mike said calmly. "Come on . . . if you've got proof I'll see it. I'm not a vicious man. You prove you are not a stowaway and I'll see what I can do for you."

"I . . . I had a wallet," Harold faltered, feeling in his coat pocket, then patting his other pockets desperately. "There was my wallet, with my cheque book and driving licence, and one or two letters."

Mike held out his hand.

"All right . . . show me. That's all I'm asking."

Harold's face was growing paler and paler as he realised that the all-important wallet was missing. He was suddenly beginning to realise that he was in a very awkward spot.

"I can't find the wallet," he finally admitted, striving hard to keep calm. "Now, listen, you've got to listen to me," and, as quickly as he could, he told how he had come aboard the trawler with his grandfather and had been accidentally locked in the fish hold. He finished by saying: "You call the crew, and I'll show you the man who took me below. He'll remember."

Mike shook his head.

"Are you trying to tell me that old Josh Jackson would bring his grandson aboard . . . and go away without him? No . . . laddie, old Josh doesn't forget people as easy as that."

"Call the crew," Harold insisted, "and I'll show you the man."

"Shall I belt him across the earhole and take him away?" Mat asked, and Mike had difficulty in repressing a smile. He shook his head.

"No, Mr. Mate . . . I'm a just man. Call the crew . . . and we'll see who it was who shut this young man in the fish hold." Then to Harold, "I hope you can find him . . . because if I discover you're just telling a pack of lies, I'll make it hard for you."

Harold gulped, but squared his shoulders as he said:

"There won't be any need for that. I'll know the man when I see him."

Mat Webber called the crew on deck, everyone except the stoker and engineer on duty below. Even the cook, an oldish man, lined up for the identification parade. The deckhands stared curiously at Harold, for the story had already gone round how he had punched Mat Webber's nose.

Harold stared anxiously at every man, but, of course,

he could not find the man who had locked him in the fish
hold. The Ship's Runner was back in the port they had left
forty minutes earlier.

Harold felt sure he was in the middle of a particularly
horrible nightmare. The wind sighed over the deck and
from upstream came the deep "wuff-wuff-wuff" of a
tugboat's siren. A seabird mewed plaintively overhead . . .
and Mike Grory was at his elbow, waiting.

"Well," Mike finally asked: "Which of them did it?"

Harold gulped, then shook his head.

Mike nodded to the waiting deckhands.

"All right, lads, you can go below." Then to Harold,
"So you were just lying to me, eh? All right, I said I'd
make it hard for you if you were. You can go below . . . as
apprentice stoker. If you work hard I'll allow you your food
and five bob a week. That's all."

He turned to walk back to the wheelhouse, but Harold
ran after him and grabbed his coat sleeve.

"I'm not going into the stinking engine-room, not for
you or anyone else," he said firmly. "Now, what do you
say to that."

Mike smiled, then turned to Mat Webber.

"Well, there you are, Mr. Mate. Looks as if he's had the
last word, eh? Oh, well . . . I don't know what your name is,
m'lad, but so long as you don't clutter up the deck I don't
mind you staying aboard. There's only one thing you
must remember. I have bunks and food for members of
the crew . . . that's all. Those who don't work aboard this
trawler don't eat. Mr. Mate . . . pass the word to the cook
that this stowaway is not on the ration strength. That'll
be all."

"I'll starve before I'm beaten by you," Harold snapped.

"That's all right to us," Mike said gently. "You'll have every opportunity of starving. We'll be away for three weeks, and they tell me that sea air gives people a good appetite." And, puffing at his cigar, he made his way back to the wheelhouse, leaving Harold standing on deck, pale-faced and angry, undecided what to do next.

CHAPTER THREE

HAROLD LOSES THE FIRST ROUND

THERE WAS a chuckle from Mat Webber as he followed Mike to the wheelhouse, and the sound made Harold grit his teeth together.

"The rotters," he muttered. "By gosh, I'll make them both pay when I get ashore. When Grandfather hears of this he'll just about blow up. I wouldn't be in their shoes, then." The thought gave him a momentary feeling of satisfaction, but it lasted only for a moment. Then he walked to the starboard bulwark and stared moodily at the flat landscape of Lincolnshire. They had just passed the entrance to Immingham docks, and he wondered for a moment whether he dare dive overboard and swim for it. The distance, he decided, would be less than a mile.

"I could do it," he decided, and began to unlace his shoes.

He had, however, forgotten that he was in full view of the wheelhouse, and by the time he had kicked off his shoes Mat Webber was by his side, grinning.

"Not thinking of desertin' ship, are you?" he asked, taking a grip on Harold's right arm. "I wouldn't do that, m'lad. Not as we care tuppence whether you leave or not. Trouble is, if you jump over the side we're bound to stop and lower a boat. If ever you learns to read, and takes the trouble to read the rules of seamanship and navigation, you'll see as it says anybody who sees a man go over the side has got to sing out ' Man overboard '. Then he's got to throw a lifebuoy. The next thing is stopping the ship and lowering a boat."

"You needn't worry about me," Harold snapped, "I can look after myself, and . . ."

"We're not worryin' about you, m'lad," Mat assured him, "but if you happened to be drowned, and we hadn't lowered a boat, there'd be awkward questions, see. Now, put them fancy shoes on or I'll give you a fourpenny one across the jaw."

Harold glared at the mate, and if he had not been in such a furious temper he might have seen the twinkle in Mat's china-blue eyes. As it was, all he saw was a powerfully built man who seemed to be itching for an excuse to give him a fourpenny one in return for the blow Harold had given him earlier.

"I don't reckon to tell anybody twice," Mat warned, "but as you're new to the *Annie*, I'll tell you once more . . . get them shoes on, or I'll clout you on the earhole."

Harold reluctantly began to put on his shoes, while Mat stood on one side, grinning, and rolling a cigarette. By the time the Mate returned to the wheelhouse the river was widening, and there were patches of shoal water between the *Annie* and the shore, making swimming to land almost an impossibility. Harold's last chance seemed to have gone.

Not until they were at the mouth of the river, and beginning to feel the first kick of the sea, did another idea occur to the "stowaway." The white buildings on Spurn Point suddenly reminded him that the trawler carried a wireless set. If he could get a radio message to his grandfather everything might yet be smoothed out. The *Blackball Annie* would be ordered to the nearest port and he would be put ashore.

He made his way to the wheelhouse, but was ordered back on deck, and from an open window Mike Grory listened to his request that a radio message be sent to old Josh Jackson.

"Got any money?" Mike asked. "It costs hard cash to send radio messages."

Harold felt in his trousers' pocket and brought out a handful of silver. He took it up to the wheelhouse and laid it on the little corner ledge.

"Take what is necessary out of that," he said coldly, and then, with an edge to his voice added: "And you can keep what is left for your trouble."

Mike Grory's mouth tightened a little at the insult. Then he smiled, but it was a grim smile.

"Listen, shaver, you won't get any change out of me by taking that attitude. I'm skipper, and there's men three times your age, and ten times as good, don't talk to me like that. You're piling up a lot of trouble for yourself."

"I'll risk that," was Harold's curt retort. "You send that message, and then we'll see who's likely to be in trouble. I can tell you now . . . it won't be me."

Mike smiled. He knew already what the answer to any radio message would be, but decided to let Harold wait, and hope.

"I'll get the radio man to send it after we've had dinner," he said. "I'm hungry, and I daresay he is, too. I don't suppose you are . . . or you'd have gone down to the stoke-hold to earn your dinner. Write out your message . . . then get back on deck. You're in the way here."

The message was written out, then Harold went back on deck. He was feeling very hungry, nor did sight of the deckhands coming from the aft cabin, lighting cigarettes after a substantial meal, make him feel less hungry. They were smoking, chatting, picking their teeth, and all obviously well fed.

An hour passed, and now the *Annie* was kicking her heels to a slight chop on the water. She was heading nor'-nor'-west, her landmark Flamborough Head.

Harold asked at the wheelhouse if a reply had come, but it had not. Slowly the afternoon wore on, with hunger now beginning to make Harold feel more miserable than ever.

Tea-time came, and at the cry "Come and get it!" from the cook, the deckhands trooped aft again for another meal. Harold had eaten nothing since breakfast. When the crew were returning to the fo'c'sle again one of them jokingly asked the "stowaway":

"Coming all the way with us, cully?"

Harold gave a contemptuous sniff, but made no other reply.

The sun went down over the land in a blaze of sullen glory, turning to ruddy purple banks of stormy-looking clouds. A chill wind began to blow, and Harold was soon shivering. His sports vest, light silk shirt, canary pullover and sports jacket were not exactly the right attire for a sea voyage, even in summer. The North Sea can be a cold place at any time of the year.

Forced by hunger and desperation, he risked the wrath of Mat Webber, whom he could see beside the helmsman, and climbed to the wheelhouse. Mat was rolling a cigarette. He never seemed to be doing anything else. The mate had recently had his tea and relieved Mike Grory. Mat sucked at his teeth, then spat a fragment of meat on to the floorboards.

"I always feel better tempered after a meal," he said,

ignoring Harold who had just closed the wheelhouse door.
"I don't know why it is; unless it's 'cause we have a cook
who *can* cook. Not like some grub-spoilers I've known.
That cottage-pie he served at tea was marvellous . . . better
than the ones Mother used to make. Meat like chicken, and
the gravy . . . aaah!"

Harold could feel the saliva beginning to flow into his
mouth. The very mention of food was enough to heighten
the feeling of hunger which gnawed at him. Desperately
he turned to Mat and asked:

"Have you had any reply to my radio message?"

"Radio message?" Mat frowned, sucked at his teeth again,
and then, pretending to remember said: "Oh, yes . . . yes
he has. The skipper's got it, I think." He thumped with a
sea-booted foot on the hatchway which led from wheelhouse
to chartroom, where the skipper lived, and called out. "You
did get a reply from Josh Jackson, didn't you? . . . about this
here stowaway. His lordship wants the answer."

Faintly from below came the command:

"Send him down here."

Mat opened the trapdoor, revealing a flight of seven steps
which gave access to the chartroom. He jerked his thumb
as a signal to Harold to go down, then he allowed the
trapdoor to fall just too late to bang Harold's head.

Mike Grory was seated at a small table. There was a
comfortable looking bunk along one wall, and in the ceiling
a compass, so that even when in bed the skipper could see
at a glance whether the *Annie* was kept on course. There
were rolls of maps, and other sea-going impedimenta; a
large First Aid box, a box marked "Rockets". It seemed as
if this chartroom was the storeroom of the trawler, as well
as the skipper's quarters.

Harold saw it all, but hardly noticed it. Mike was having his evening meal. There was a jug of delicious smelling coffee. There was a deep-plate pie, the meat luscious looking and the gravy thick and brown. There was a portion of jam roll and a small jug of golden custard. Harold knew then just how hungry he was. He could have sat down and wolfed everything in sight. Instead he took the slip of paper Mike held out to him, and read:

"Do not understand message. Grandson playing tennis with friends. Dancing to-night. Stowaway obviously an impostor. Make him work his passage. Jackson."

The words seemed to dance a jig before Harold's eyes. It couldn't be true. Yet . . . if it wasn't true, if this message was a fake, how did whoever had written the message know that he should have been playing tennis that afternoon, and due to go to a dance that evening? The message *must* have come from his grandfather.

Mike Grory looked at his watch.

"I'll give you another chance," he said coldly. "We change watches at six. You can go on as assistant stoker with Sam, and I'll . . ."

"I'll do nothing of the kind," the words were out almost before Harold realised what he was saying.

"All right. Up you go. And remember . . . there's neither bunk nor food aboard this ship for those who won't work. Go on . . . get moving. You can go out at the door. They don't want you in the wheelhouse."

Harold went out, and stood by the port rail, staring hungrily shorewards. He could see a cluster of lights, like tiny jewels, away towards the horizon. He fancied they were at Withernsea. It was only a few miles away, but it might just as well have been in another world. He was a prisoner aboard the *Annie* just as surely as if he had been held in iron chains and locked behind a heavy iron-studded door. Even the thought that eventually he would have a satisfying revenge on both skipper and mate did not ease his hunger, or lighten his growing misery. For the first time in his life he knew what real hunger meant.

The twilight deepened, and soon there were stars out. There was just a faint light in the wheelhouse, enough to light the compass. The riding lights were on, and the port light cast a blood-red glow on the waves. The trawler was beginning to roll now as a cross-wind blew, and the little ship was suddenly a very lonely place.

In the fo'c'sle there were some dozen or more deckhands. There was a deckhand at the wheel, and with him either the mate or the skipper. Down below, the engineer and the stoker could speak to one another; but Harold was alone. There was no bed or bunk for him; no food; no one he could talk to. No one was worrying about him. He could fall overboard and be drowned and no one would bother. He began to feel very sorry for himself.

Finally, just before ten o'clock, he made his way cautiously to the galley, determined to get food at all costs. He was as thirsty as he was hungry, for he had had nothing since coming aboard.

The dimly lighted galley was empty. The coal fire was glowing, and comfortably warm. On a hot-plate stood what looked like a portable oven, and a big black saucepan was perched half on and half off the fire. From it came an appetising odour.

Deciding that the cook was probably in his bunk, Harold lifted the lid of the saucepan. It contained something tied up in a rag, probably a suet dumpling. The portable oven, however, held what Harold was looking for, a pie. The crust was richly brown, and the odour was the most appetising Harold had ever known. There was the combined smell of potatoes, meat, gravy and onions, a dish for a king if he happened to be as hungry as Harold Jackson.

Just as Harold was about to take the pie out, using an oven cloth so that he would not burn his fingers, a voice from the doorway made him jump nervously.

"Hoi . . . hoi . . . keep thy fingers from picking and stealing, and thy lips from speaking guile."

Harold turned quickly to face the cook. He was an oldish man, with straggly grey hair, a bedraggled looking chef's cap, and eyes which were very sad. Shaking his head, he pushed past Harold and closed the oven door, at the same time saying:

"He what takes what isn't his'n, when he's cotched he's sent to prison. You gets no food out of here, young shaver. I've had my orders about you."

"But look, I'm absolutely starving," Harold insisted. "I've not had a bite since breakfast. What difference does it make to you? There's plenty of food aboard, surely, and nobody would ever know."

The cook shook his head slowly.

"If I could do somethin' for you, laddie, I would," he said gently, then paused to rub his hand across his unshaven chin. "But when you comes aboard a ship . . . whether she's an old trawler like this, or one as big as the *Queen Mary*, there's one chap in command. They might call him a Commodore, an Admiral, or even ' The Bloke ', as they does aboard a trawler, but he's the boss. If he gives an order, you obeys it, or there's trouble."

"But, listen," Harold pleaded. "I'm the grandson of Mr.

Josh Jackson, who owns this trawler . . . yes, and a dozen other trawlers bigger than this. If you help me I promise you this . . . once we get ashore again I'll see you get a better job. I give you my word of honour I will."

The old man shook his head.

"There's an old saying, laddie: ' Obey orders if you break owners.' You may be the owner's grandson, I know nothin' about that. I do know that when Mike Grory gives an order aboard this ship . . . you obeys it."

"Couldn't you give me a bite? Just a mouthful?" Harold pleaded. "I'm starving."

"I could stuff you that full of Shepherd's pie it'd be trickling out o' your ears," the cook replied, "and if I'd my way I would. But then I don't have my way aboard the *Annie*. I does what the skipper orders. Now listen to me . . . I'll just give you a word of advice. Take it or leave it. I know young folks never reckon much of advice given by the old 'uns. You do what Mike Grory says. You can't beat him while you're aboard the *Annie*. Here, he's like a little tin god. He's boss . . . boss of everybody and everythin'. He could clap you in irons if he were so minded. Now, you be sensible. Go and tell him you're willing to work, and I'll put a meal out for you as you'll never forget."

"No, I won't give in to him," Harold insisted. "I'll starve first."

"It's easier said than done," the cook said, but Harold did not hear him; he had turned and stamped out on to the deck once more.

In the short time he had been in the cook's galley, however, a distinct change had come over the scene. The night wind had a keener bite, and the *Annie* was rolling more. Spray was flying through the air, stinging the skin; while a distinct slop of water was being shipped at the waist, and it sloshed towards the stern in a foot-high wave before rushing with a throaty gurgling out through the scupper pipes.

Harold shivered, and tried to persuade himself that he could stick it out. He hated submitting to anyone, least of all to the black-jowled Mike Grory who was "tin god" aboard the wallowing *Annie*. As long as he could remember, Harold had done just what he had said he would do. His grandmother had been indulgent, and, as old Josh Jackson had suggested to Grory, he had been somewhat spoiled. Nevertheless, he was in a different world now. Here there was no servant to answer his ring on a bell, no dainty food to be had whenever he wished. He was cold, hungry, and had nowhere to go . . . unless he admitted defeat and agreed to work as a member of the crew.

Suddenly he made up his mind. He splashed through the water rushing along the deck to the stern, climbed the wheelhouse ladder, and stared defiantly at Mike Grory who had recently relieved the mate.

"You win," Harold said curtly. "I'm hungry, and if I can't eat until I work, then I'll work."

"Now that's talking sense," Mike agreed, nodding amiably. "You do your best for me and the ship, in return I'll see you get to know something about trawling and trawlers. You'll not find it . . ."

"You can cut out the sermon," Harold said rudely, at which the deckhand at the wheel turned and gaped. Not many people dared talk to Mike Grory like that and certainly not in his own wheelhouse.

Grory had been feeling for a match for his pipe, but at Harold's remark he looked up, nodded, and said quietly:

"I see; you won't admit defeat gracefully. Very well, I was going to send you for'ard for a night's rest; but I can change my mind quick enough, m'lad. You can take this note to the cook. He'll give you a meal, and when you've eaten you go down into the stokehold and do the one-to-eight night watch. If *you* are tough, you can have it tough."

He tore a scrap of paper from a pad, wrote swiftly, and handed the message to Harold.

"That'll get you a meal. It puts you on the ship's roster. You're an apprentice stoker now. If you won't be nice about this business, you can have the rough side. Go on . . . get moving."

CHAPTER FOUR

PRIDE OF THE JACKSONS

APPRENTICE STOKER! Harold went colder than ever at the thought of going down below. He had spent a few moments in the stokehold when the *Annie* lay at her moorings in the fish dock. He had wondered then how any man could stay down there, for the stokehold was small. It had seemed terribly hot even then, and the fires had only been purring softly, like contented cats. What it would be like now, when the engines were lapping up steam and the fires would be roaring away at full blast he could hardly imagine. It was a frightening prospect.

"Scared?" Mike asked, and struck a match for his pipe. If Harold admitted that he was frightened the skipper of the *Annie* would have relented. Though he was playing the part of a tough, and bullying skipper, Mike Grory was beginning to have a sneaking admiration for this slim young landlubber. It took plenty of guts for anyone to stay without food or drink for more than twelve hours. It needed courage for anyone to defy a skipper as Harold had done. Mike had already decided that this pale-faced stripling was indeed a real chip off the old block. He had the courage and will-power of his grandfather. Once some of the cockiness had been knocked out of him, Mike felt sure that Harold Jackson would turn out to be a grand youngster. He waited patiently for the reply to his single-word question: "Scared?"

Harold's stiff-necked pride doomed him to a night in the

searing heat of the stokehold. He *was* scared; horribly scared; but he refused to let this tall, burly, and, as he thought, bullying, skipper know of his fear. His lip curled a little in a contemptuous sneer as he said:

"I'm not scared of anything aboard this ship . . . or anyone."

They were brave words, but he could not keep a slight tremor from his voice.

"I'll see if you've changed your mind by morning," Mike suggested, and smiled as Harold turned on his heel, swung open the wheelhouse door, and clattered down to the deck.

He gave Grory's note to the cook, who was dozing on a locker in the aft cabin, waiting for his dough to rise. Aboard the *Annie*, bread was baked every day, and there were eighteen in the crew; eighteen hungry men, and they ate a lot of bread.

The cook read the note Harold gave him, then nodded.

"Sit ye down, lad. I won't be more'n a minute or so."

Harold accepted the invitation gladly. His shoes were sodden, his once immaculate flannels were soaked to the knees, and their knife-like creases gone for ever. He felt cold right through to the bone, and remained crouched by the cabin stove until the cook came back again.

At Helmshore, Josh Jackson's twelve-bedroomed house, meals were taken from the finest china. The cutlery was silver, and food was served with noiseless efficiency. Harold's first meal aboard the *Annie* was rather different.

The cabin being in the stern, the thump and vibration of the ship's propeller could be felt distinctly. As for the cabin table . . . deckhands by the score seemed to have cut their initials in the woodwork, while the table itself was divided into little partitions by three-inch-high pieces of wood. This was to prevent plates sliding about in rough weather as the *Annie* wallowed and rolled.

The cutlery was steel, big and strong. The dinner plate which the cook set before Harold was also big and thick, but it was what the plate contained which made Harold's eyes shine. There was a great wedge of shepherd's pie, with three thick potato cakes, each the size of a saucer, holding the pie down. Topping everything was a fried egg. Had that been set before Harold at any other time he would have been disgusted. Now he was delighted.

"Sing out if you want any more," the cook said, and winked as he added: "I might be able to find something else."

Before Harold had finished, the cook was down again. This time there was a liberal helping of suet dumpling, thickly smeared with yellow custard. Then came a pint pot of steaming coffee.

By the time Harold had finished he was warm again. Warm, and feeling happy, and sleepy. When the chief engineer and the stoker came in about half-past twelve, prior to going on duty, the "stowaway" was fast asleep on the locker.

They wakened him about ten minutes to one, for they changed over at one o'clock, and would be on continuous duty for seven hours, being relieved at eight o'clock next morning.

"You'd better dump your coat an' shirt," the stoker said. "Where we're goin' it'll be warm enough without a jacket. At least I never needs one ... and I dessay my blood's thinner than yours."

They climbed the ladder from the cabin to the passage

above. To the right was the door leading on to the black, wet deck. To the left, the opening to the engine-room.

Getting down to the level of the engine-room was tricky. The ladder was steel, and perpendicular. Years of use had worn the tread off the rungs, so that the metal was smooth and shiny. What was more, it had a thin skim of grease on it, and to make matters more difficult the *Annie* was now plunging and bucketing like a mad thing. The cross-wind was making her bury her bows every few seconds. She was shipping it green, taking dark masses of water over her starboard rail and shaking herself like a duck as she flung the water over her stern and portside.

Harold watched Bill Howson, the engineer, turn round, face the ladder, and then vanish. He had slid down, his feet on the side supports, his hands firmly hooked on the single handrail. The way he did it made the action look easy.

Sam, the stoker, a thin, wiry little man who looked far too puny to manage three fires in the big, marine-type boiler, followed his chief's example, leaving Harold standing at the top, looking helplessly, and anxiously, down into the engine-room. The rolling and plunging of the *Annie* was making him feel slightly dizzy.

The steel plates of the engine-room looked a very long way down, and what was more, the engines themselves looked too near the foot of the ladder. The three shiny piston rods of the high-, medium-, and low-pressure cylinders plunged up and down, up and down, while beneath them the crankshaft whirled madly in the dark depths of the crankpit. It all looked very strange and frightening.

Down there, the second engineer was handing over to Bill Howson, and lighting a cigarette as he discussed some point. The stoker coming off duty was having a word with Sam, and not one of them seemed concerned whether Harold went down there or not.

"You've got to go down," Harold told himself. "You can't let them see you are scared. They'd laugh themselves sick if you funked it."

The *Annie* seemed to be rolling worse than ever, and almost any newcomer could have been excused for refusing point blank to try the journey down that narrow steel ladder. Harold's pride helped him down. He had the feeling that the four men below were discussing him, and probably watching to see what he would do.

Turning round as he had seen the engineer and Sam do, he grasped the shiny handrail, put one foot on the top rung of the ladder and steadied himself. The trawler swayed over to starboard, then for a second she swung back on to an even keel. Harold took what he thought was his chance; an opportunity to scuttle down the ladder before the trawler began to roll again.

It was a mistake. Only an experienced man can hurry down a perpendicular ladder aboard a small craft when there is a rough sea running. Harold was just four rungs down when the *Annie* heaved up on the starboard as a great wave slid under her bows and travelled along her weather side.

What happened next took only a second or so from beginning to end. Harold was thrown off-balance. One foot slid off the ladder rung, and he made a desperate lunge to save himself. For a moment he hung by one hand, screaming, but he could not hold himself. The ladder rail was as greasy as the ladder rungs.

Down he went, his hand sliding along the polished rail. He was thrown away from the ladder as the trawler heaved more and more . . . thrown towards the engines, and his hand lost its grip.

His foot struck the guard rail around the engine-pit, and for an instant he remained poised there, teetering for balance. Below him was the crank-pit, the crankshaft turning busily, the pistons driving down, up, down, up, the big ends threshing in the sump of oily bilge-water at the bottom. Anyone falling into the sump would be mangled to pulp in seconds.

Though it all happened in a moment or so, to Harold it seemed long-drawn-out, like a slow-motion film. He caught a glimpse of the agonised expression of the face of the second engineer. He realised the man was beginning to move towards him, lifting his hands, meaning to help. Then Harold was falling, falling into the crankpit, and the outstretched hands were too late.

Harold did try to help himself. He clutched at the nearest thing, but it was the sleek, shining piston rod, coated with a thin film of oil. No human hand could hold on to that. He sprawled on to the big-end. It took him down, swiftly, smoothly. When it came up, having completed half an arc, then it would trap him, crush him . . . crush him to death. He could not stop it, for it was being driven on by two hundred pounds of steam to the square inch in the workmanlike cylinder above.

Looking up he could see a horrified face staring down at him. The face of the second engineer. He was a youngish man, and there was an oily smear across his cheek and the bridge of his nose. Harold had just time to realise that two hands were stretched down towards him when the motion of the crankshaft stopped with a sudden, unexpected jerk.

Bill Howson, with more than twenty years' experience in ships' engine-rooms, had long ago learned to do the right thing at the right moment. He had made no attempt to stop Harold falling into the sump. He had not been sure the stowaway would fall into the sump, but he had done the right thing, jumping to the steam throttle, and shutting off immediately.

Harold was hauled out of the engine-pit. He was quite incapable of helping himself, and as he was laid on the greasy plates there was a thin, piping whistle from the voice-tube which connects engine-room and wheelhouse. Whoever was in the wheelhouse wanted to know what was wrong, and why the engines had been stopped.

Bill Howson jerked a thumb towards the steam throttle, and while the second engineer re-started the engines, he went to the voice tube and gave some explanation to the man in the wheelhouse. When he came back, wiping his hands on a wad of engine-room waste, he was grinning.

"That were old Mat," he said, "and I reckon it just about put the wind-up him good and proper. Thought we'd bust something. It's blowing up for a gale on top, and I reckon he were worried."

"We nearly did bust something," the second engineer said feelingly, while he chafed Harold's right wrist. "Cor, Bill, I've never seen anybody nearer getting a one-way ticket to Eternity than this kid."

Bill nodded.

"Aye, it were a near do," he admitted. "Has Sam gone for something?"

Sam had gone for a cup of strong tea, and Harold lay and listened while the man discussed the near-accident. He did not feel annoyed when the engineer mentioned that the "stowaway" had tried to kid the skipper that he was the grandson of the owner of the trawler. The three men chuckled at that, but Harold was not annoyed. For the time being he felt as if he was in another world. The shock of his near-death had temporarily stopped his mind working.

Then Sam came back, bringing a pint pot of strong, sweet tea. The second engineer and the other stoker went off duty, and while Sam went through to attend to his fires, Bill Howson got Harold into a sitting position, his back to the tool locker, and there he coaxed him into drinking.

"Now there's nowt wrong with you, kid," Bill kept saying. "Not a blessed thing. Them flannel bags you're wearin' won't be the same again, I'll admit, but you'd have got them mucky in the stokehold anyway. You're not hurt; not a scratch."

Harold listened. He drank the tea, and then quite suddenly he began to cry. Bill Howson had seen cases of shock before and he rose from his kneeling position, saying curtly:

"Get up, you big, soft lout. What are you blubbing for? You haven't a scratch on you that I can see. Get into the stokehold or I'll give you summat to start bawling about."

It was probably the finest antidote for shock and near-hysterics he could have given to Harold. It stopped his sobs in less than a minute. He was quivering inwardly, but pride made him fight for control. To be called a "big, soft lout" hit him in his tenderest spot, his pride. Harold Jackson had always secretly prided himself on being a little bit tougher than other fellows of his own age.

The *Annie* was rolling badly now, and, when Harold got to his feet, he had to hang on to a tool-rack, bolted to the side of the ship, to get his balance. Dipping her bows under every minute or so, the trawler was lifting her stern so that her screw came out of the water, allowing it to race, and shaking the engines as the labouring piston rods seemed suddenly to go mad, shooting up and down with eye-dazzling speed until the stern dipped again, and once more the screw bit water. It was not good for the engines, and Bill Howson moved across to the controls, ready to shut off steam the moment the screw came out of water, and equally quick to open up again when the racing stopped.

Harold stood for a moment and stared at the burly engineer. He looked more like a navvy than anything else. To that man, Harold owed his life, yet he felt no gratitude just then. The hot, sweet tea had worked wonders, but he was still suffering from shock, and all he could think of was that he hated Bill Howson. Hated him for taunting him with that sneering, "You big, soft lout." Without a word of thanks, Harold turned to the narrow passage which connects engine-room and stokehold.

Bill Howson turned just in time to see him disappearing from view.

"He'd have been better for an hour's sleep," Howson muttered, and might have followed Harold into the gloom to order him up to the fo'c'sle for the rest of the watch, but the trawler gave an extra wicked slew at that moment, and Bill had to shut off again. By the time the *Annie* was running easier—Mike Grory having agreed to turn her into the wind for a while, Harold was forgotten. Bill had other things to think of.

In the stokehold, Harold stood for a moment and looked fearfully about him. Sam Pickup was throwing coal into the port fire, his thin face and beaky nose lit up by the yellow glare from the open firebox. Sweat was dripping from his chin, yet, despite the rolling of the ship, each shovel-load of fuel went straight to its mark, the coal scattering thinly over the roaring flames, and firing almost immediately in the great heat.

Slamming the firebox door shut, Sam wiped the sweat from his face and neck with the sweat-rag about his wrist. Then he smiled as he realised Harold had joined him. He brought the stub of a cigarette from behind his ear, touched it against one of the nearest firebars, and in a moment he was smoking. Harold gaped! If the heat was so great under there, it struck him as amazing that Sam had not winced. His hands must have been iron hard.

"What's your name, cully?" Sam was asking. "I'm Sam Pickup."

"Jackson. Harold *Jackson*."

The name Jackson, even though Harold had put emphasis on it, did not seem to strike any chord with Sam, for he merely nodded. Then he pointed to a cane basket on four small wheels.

"Look, take that and fill it with coal from the fish hold. Open that door, and go through the tunnel. It runs through the bunkers. We reckons to keep about twenty-thirty tons o' coal in the fish holds . . . and we've got to use that first, so's we're cleaned up for when we start fishin'. There's a torch up there. Use my spare shovel."

He opened a door, some three feet high and the same distance wide. It looked blacker than the Pit, and Harold hesitated.

"You . . . you mean . . . go . . . through there?" he asked, and there was a quiver in his voice.

Sam laughed.

"That's right," and then, for the second time that night Harold faced the question: "You're not scared, are you?"

Grabbing torch, shovel, and the rope handle of the basket, Harold stepped cautiously into the tunnel. He had to bend almost double. He was scared, but he was determined no one should know it.

The moment he had dragged the basket into the tunnel, the door was slammed shut, cutting out the ruddy glow from beneath the three furnaces, and the darkness was like that known by a blind man, thick, impenetrable, solid. Harold forgot he had a torch in his hand. Fear and anger were mixed as he pushed past the basket and tried to open the door again. This was just a trick to frighten him. Well, he'd jolly well show them. He pushed the door, but it was firm, immovable, not giving the slightest.

Sam Pickup had locked him in!

CHAPTER FIVE

SCALDING STEAM

HAROLD hammered frantically on the door, shouting at the top of his voice for Sam to let him out. In that small tunnel, he could hear all kinds of queer, frightening sounds. The creak of metal, the squeaking of loose rivets as the trawler strained to the smashing impact of each heavy sea. The sound of the torch on the iron door was flung back at him like thunder.

"Let me out!" he screamed. "Open the door . . . open it, I tell you! Open it!"

Suddenly, as he was starting to hammer at the ironwork again, the door did open, and he almost fell into Sam Pickup's arms. The wiry little stoker steadied Harold, looked at him wonderingly, then asked:

"What's the matter? There's nowt wrong. I shut the door so's I wouldn't bang myself on it when I were getting coal."

"But you locked me in," Harold stammered, suddenly feeling ashamed. "I . . . I . . ."

Sam shook his head and pointed to the inside of the door. "There's the latch. Couldn't you see it? You'd a torch."

Harold looked at the torch in his hand. The glass was broken, the front battered out of shape.

"I . . . dropped it," he lied, "and . . . it went out."

Sam found him a small oil lamp, and guided Harold through the tunnel into the fish hold. The first two holds were filled with ice, the midship's hold with coal. Harold spent the next hour and a half dragging baskets of coal through to the stokehold.

When he had rested, Sam insisted on teaching him how to fire the boiler. The heat, as each firebox door was opened in turn, seemed to shrivel Harold's skin, and, even though Sam gave him wet rags to put around his hands, he kept looking to see if blisters, burn-blisters were forming.

Half-way through the night, when two of the fires were purring away like giant cats, Sam pointed to a " slice" the tool with which he had just cleared the firebars of port and starboard fires.

" I'm just nipping up topsides for a can of water," he said. " See if you can break the clinker in that middle fire. I'll not be more than a few minutes."

With that he opened his cigarette tin—once it had held cough lozenges—lit up, and left the stokehold.

Harold looked at the "slice". It was a steel rod, about an inch thick and some ten or twelve feet long. On one end was a ringed handle, on the other a flat metal rod stuck up. This was the actual "slice", and when thrust upwards beneath the firebars, broke the fused clinker which was preventing air getting to the fire, and so slowing up combustion.

Sam had "sliced" the other two fires with ease. Or, at least, it had looked easy. The trouble was, Harold thought ruefully, that everything the puny little stoker did looked easy.

Harold shook his head. He was beginning to wonder if he was as fit as he had thought. He could play tennis by the hour and never weary. He was a powerful swimmer, and a first-class oarsman. His friends envied him his strength, and his staying-powers. Yet, in the short time he had been down in the stokehold, Harold was beginning to wonder just what "fitness" was. If he was fit, then Sam Pickup, middle-aged, thin and scrawny, was a miracle of toughness and fitter than ten fiddles. He had been throwing coal on to the fires for three and a half hours, and though sweat had poured out of him, he showed no signs of weariness or fatigue.

"Well," Harold decided, "I suppose if he can do it . . . I can. I'll show them all that I'm as good as they are; not that Sam's done any boasting. I think I rather like him."

Dipping his sweat rags in the bucket of lukewarm water, he wrapped them about his hands and wrists. Then he picked up the slice. He gave a dejected whistle of amazement. Sam had picked it up as if it might have been made of cane, or balsa wood. To Harold's amazement, it was a terrific weight, sixty or seventy pounds, he imagined.

Staggering a little, as the trawler did a sudden jig and dance as an extra heavy sea thrust at her, he somehow managed to get the fireman's slice under the middle fire. He got the point upright, then tried to force it through the fused mass of glowing clinker which was choking the firebars. When Sam had done that, the clinker had parted with ease. Now, for some unknown reason, the clinker just refused to break up.

By the time he had broken it, the rags protecting wrists and arms were almost dry, and terribly hot. His eyes were aching from staring into the glare of the red-hot firebars, and the slice had somehow got jammed!

Jerking, banging, whimpering in temper, Harold fought to get the slice free. The air was roaring through the broken-up clinker, and the fire was burning better . . . much better, and the heat was increasing. Harold half expected the sweat rags on his hands to burst into flame any moment.

Then, quite unexpectedly, the slice came free, and the handle came into his midriff with a painful jar. At that he lost his temper completely. He pulled the slice from beneath the middle firebox, and flung it from him. The ten-inch end was almost white hot, having been kept in the fire much too long. For a moment the slice stood on its rounded handle, like some silly stokehold imitation of tossing the caber, then it leaned forward and clanked against the boiler. The glowing end somehow insinuated itself in the slit of the brass shield which guards the water gauge.

That gauge is connected at the top to the steam in the boiler and at the bottom to the water. It shows how much water there is thrumming away in the black monster which feeds invisible steam to the ever-hungry engines. The pressure within that narrow plate glass tube was just on the two hundred pounds per square inch mark . . . the same as the steam pressure in the boiler.

The sharp blow from the red-hot end of the slice broke the glass. There was a whip-like crack as the gauge glass dissolved into hundreds of minute pieces, and one small piece, with diabolical speed, struck the swinging electric light. That popped, and the stokehold was lit only by the ruddy glow from beneath the three fires.

Harold cringed instinctively at the first report, then cowered in terror at the scream of high-pressure steam escaping from a small vent. Scalding water was spitting out, too, from the bottom of the gauge, dropping like red-hot rain.

Looking up for a moment, Harold was almost petrified by the sight of a great cloud of vapour which hid the top of the boiler completely. He did not look up for more than a couple of seconds, for minute drops of scalding water forced him to look away.

He panicked.

What had happened, he could not guess. For all he knew, the boiler might be about to blow up, in which case he would meet a terrible death. There was only one thing to do, and he did it. He ran.

Unfortunately, such was his panic, he ran the wrong way. He happened to be facing away from the passage which led to the engine-room, and so, instead of getting out of the stokehold, he merely ran into a solid iron wall of plates . . . the side of the ship.

Frantically he fumbled for a moment or so, wondering where the exit was. Then he realised what he had done, and turned. He did not run now. By the glow from the three fireboxes, he could see the cloud of steam, and he could feel the heat, growing greater every moment. To reach safety, he had to pass that middle spot, above which the steam was blowing off, and from which was dropping that fine, scalding rain.

For a moment he hesitated, nerving himself for the dash; but before he could move something happened. There was a brilliant flash of yellow light, so vivid and unexpected that he shrank back, automatically lifting his hands to shield his eyes. He waited for the terrifying roar of an explosion, followed by a whirlwind of death-dealing pieces of tortured metal, plus the biting sting of scalding water and high-pressure steam.

Nothing happened. The stokehold did not dissolve into a chaos of tortured steel plates. There was no ear-splitting crash. The scream of escaping steam still continued, and the yellow light was still shining brilliantly when he nerved himself to open his fingers a little and peer through them.

There was something, however, which had not been in the stokehold a minute before. The yellow light was shining full on the scraggy figure of Sam Pickup.

The stoker had whipped off his sweat-stained vest and was draping it about his head and shoulders. Only then did Harold realise that the golden glare was coming from the far firebox. Sam had opened the firebox door to provide light by which to work.

The stoker worked methodically, but speedily. Once his vest was draped about his head and narrow shoulders, he pushed forward the rickety basket in which Harold had dragged the coal. He turned it over, pushed it to the middle of the boiler, and clambered on top.

The trawler was still plunging and rolling, so that Sam swayed on the unstable basket, and once had to put a hand on the front of the boiler to steady himself. Harold winced, knowing how hot the boiler front was. He did not realise then that Sam's hands were toughened by many years' work in stokeholds. They were hard and calloused.

Balancing as best he could on the basket, Sam reached up into the roaring fury of steam and scalding water, at which Harold shut his eyes in horror, sick at the thought of what must be happening. Sam was being scalded; he was risking his life; his sight; not because he was forced to do it. It was part of his normal duty to see that work in the stokehold went smoothly.

A few seconds later, the scream of escaping steam and water was cut to half. The bottom cock, from which was spurting scalding water, had been turned to the horizontal, shutting it. A moment later the *Annie* gave an awkward lurch, and Sam lost his balance. His hand had been fumbling for the steam cock, and to reach it he had to stand on tiptoe. His hand missed the brass cock, and then the trawler swayed.

The basket went one way, Sam the other. He fell awkwardly, and lay sprawled across a heap of coal, face down.

Harold forgot his fears. Steam was still screeching into the air; the heat was growing almost unbearable; but he had no thought of running away now. He jumped to his feet and ran across to the little stoker. At the back of his mind was a sudden awful fear that Sam had been blinded.

"Sam . . . Sam . . . what is it? Are you hurt? Tell me . . . quick. What can I do?" He turned Sam over, and raised him to a sitting position.

Sam's dirt-smeared face was bathed in the golden glory of light from the starboard firebox. His beak-like nose was cut, and a thin trickle of blood was beginning to make a channel through the coal dust. There was a small scar on his forehead, and for a moment he stared blankly at Harold. Then he lifted a hand to his forehead, and suddenly seemed to remember where he was. He began to struggle to get to his feet.

"Gimme a hand, cully," he mumbled. "I've gotta get that steam shut off. We're losin' pressure, an' old Bill don't like that."

"You can't . . . go up there . . . again," Harold protested, but Sam merely turned to stare at him, a queer little smile on his face.

"Can't, did you say? Lor, you wait an' hear what Bill Howson will say if we lose our steam pressure. Look, we're droppin' away now," and he pointed to the steam pressure gauge, half-hidden by the billowing clouds of scalding vapour. The needle was quivering at one-seventy-two, and dropping back in little jerky twitches.

Sam pushed the shaky basket in place once more, and, with Harold to steady him, climbed up. Once again the stoker was reaching up into the screaming horror of escaping steam. Harold felt as if he was cooking down below, for the stokehold had grown steadily hotter and hotter as it filled with scalding vapour. How Sam was enduring it he could not imagine. Yet, after a minute, the howling screech grew less .. less, and then died away into a whisper. Then that, too, was shut off. In the silence which followed, the thrumming of the boiler, and the roaring purr of the fires seemed almost comforting.

Harold helped Sam off the basket, and, as he did so, the raucous voice of Bill Howson was heard demanding:

"What's going on in here?"

Bill had left his steam throttle for a few moments to find out why the shrill whistle of escaping steam had kept on so long. He slammed the firebox door shut, but jerked it open again at once when he realised the electric light was out.

"Well, what's been going on?" Bill demanded, addressing his question to Harold, who was gingerly taking the sodden, and still hot, vest from about Sam's head and shoulders. In no mood to answer what he thought were silly questions, Harold said crisply:

"Sam's been badly scalded. He'll have to be got ashore to a doctor. If you'll help him into the engine-room, I'll go and tell the skipper."

Bill stared for a moment, as if too shocked to think, then he growled:

"Tell the skipper, did you say? What are you talking about, you blamed fool. What's he got to do with it? What's the matter, Sam? Is it bad?"

Sam raised a face which looked pink and shiny in the red light from the open furnace. He managed a painful little smile as he said;

"I'll be all right in a few minutes. Them cocks is stiff ... broke a gauge glass we did, and ..."

"Look, I'm going to tell the skipper," Harold insisted, and would have pushed past Bill had the engineer not grabbed him and held him fast.

"You stop here and tend the fires," he ordered. "We're losing pressure fast. I'll see to Sam."

"He needs a doctor," Harold snapped.

"And where d'you think we'll get a doctor?" Bill demanded, scowling. "You're sailin' the North Sea, m'lad, not sitting on your backside in Hull. You grab that shovel ... you won't have enough steam to brew tea if the fires are left much longer. Go on, get moving, or I'll ... here, you brat, come here. *Come here!*"

He had pushed Harold towards the stoker's shovel, but he had not bargained for a youth as nimble and determined as Harold Jackson. People usually did as Bill Howson ordered, but Harold was different. He ducked under the engineer's outstretched arm and fled from the stokehold as if he were beginning a hundred yards sprint.

Bill swore mightily, and turned in pursuit.

As Bill re-entered the engine-room, Harold was grabbing the shiny handrail of the vertical ladder which led to the deck. Roaring out a string of ear-blistering oaths, the engineer commanded Harold to stop, but he might just as well have saved his breath. Harold Jackson had not yet learned to obey commands from anyone, and at the moment his one thought was to get to the wheelhouse and have the trawler turned towards the nearest port.

Swearing like a Billingsgate porter, Howson raced across the engine-room, made a wild leap, and managed to grab Harold's left leg.

"I'll show you . . . who's boss . . . down here," he panted. "I'm the one . . . to . . . ouch!"

He jerked Harold's left foot off the rung of the ladder, and for a second it was touch and go whether he would be brought in a tumbling heap on top of Bill. Then Harold gave a wild kick, and it was that which brought the agonised "ouch" from the burly engineer. Harold's heel caught Bill in the mouth. It puffed his lips and loosened two front teeth at the same time.

Bill let go Harold's ankle and staggered back, his hand going to his mouth, and, without waiting to see just what damage he had done, Harold fled for the deck, and, as he leapt off the last rung of the ladder, he heard Bill's mumbled threat:

"I'll murder you for this."

Bill might have made himself heard better if he had not been holding a hand to his swollen lips. The kick had been a shrewd and painful one.

Just for a moment the engineer was tempted to follow Harold, but a sudden racing of the engines as the *Annie* lifted her stern clear of the water forced him to rush across to shut off steam. By the time he had opened up again, Sam had come out of the stokehold.

In the white light of the engine-room, Sam looked a sorry mess. His face was red and shiny, his shoulders looked ready to blister any moment; but his right hand was the worst. The back was one huge blister.

"How do you feel, Sam?" Bill asked, one hand still nursing the throttle.

"Oh, not so bad," Sam said. "If I get something on my hand, I reckon I'll manage."

Bill Howson nodded.

"Well, stand by the throttle a minute. I'll have to see to them fires, or there'll be no steam at all. That young maniac doesn't seem to realise a ship's got to keep going . . . 'specially when there's a bit of a blow on. By gosh, but I'll teach him something when he comes back. Kicked me in the teeth, he did. My lips feel like puddings. Nobody kicks me in the teeth an' gets away with it. Sure you'll be all right?"

Sam nodded, and grinned, a queer, painful little grin which seemed to stretch the already tight and scalded skin on his face.

"I'll not be more'n five minutes," Bill assured him, and hurried through to the stokehold to feed the fires.

CHAPTER SIX

A LAMB TO THE SLAUGHTER

OUT ON THE OPEN deck, Harold winced at the cold. He had forgotten that a storm was raging, and the bitter wind almost drove him to the rail. Then a foot-high wall of water came surging down from the waist, and wet him, so that he gasped and fought for breath. Down in the stokehold, the *Annie* had seemed to be rolling wildly enough, but up here the ship was apparently trying to turn bottom up.

Even though she was half-turned into the wind, the *Annie* was shipping tons of water over her whaleback, and dark masses of water were racing along her decks. Harold was wet from head to foot before he was half-way to the wheel-house. The red port riding-light threw a crimson sheen on towering waves, striking terror into his heart. It seemed impossible that such a small vessel could ride out a storm like this.

He was scared of the storm, but the idea of turning back did not enter his head. Down below, Sam Pickup was badly scalded, and must have medical attention as soon as possible. How they would get him to port, and so to a hospital, Harold had no idea, but that he could persuade the skipper to try he was certain. Harold had led a sheltered life, and had no idea how tough trawlermen are. Injuries which they considered part of their everyday toil would have meant ambulances and hospital beds for many people living ashore.

Reaching the wheelhouse ladder, Harold clung there for a moment, while he fought to get back his breath. Above him the navigation light on the stumpy foremast was swinging in wild arcs as the *Annie* rolled and plunged. Even to watch it was to bring on a feeling of dizziness. Harold closed his eyes, shook his head, then scrambled up the steps.

He opened the door of the wheelhouse, and a heel of the ship shot him forward and on to his knees.

Mat Webber was leaning against the far corner, smoking a cigarette. The deckhand at the wheel had his feet well braced as he fought to keep his balance and at the same time hold the trawler on course.

Both men turned as a blast of icy wind swept in on them, and Mat bawled an angry command.

"Shut the door, you fool. Do you want us all wet through?"

Harold scrambled to his feet and somehow got the wheel-house door closed. He was breathing heavily, and for a moment he stared at Mat Webber, anger, scorn, even hate in his eyes. More than ever the mate of the *Annie* appeared as the typical bullying, blue-nose mate of sea stories. A partly-smoked cigarette dangled from one corner of his mouth. His powerful hands were dug deep into the pockets of his heavy duffle coat, and all he seemed concerned about was that the door should be closed quickly to prevent driving rain and spray from wetting him.

Almost beside himself with rage, it was a moment or so before Harold could find words. He could not get out of his mind's eye a picture of poor Sam Pickup, scalded and in pain. Scalded, but not complaining. It made Harold writhe to think that Mat Webber could be so blind as not to realise that something dreadful must have happened to bring someone up from below on a night like this.

"You'd better call the captain," Harold finally managed to say, and his voice sounded strange, hard and hoarse. "You've got to get to the nearest port as quick as you can ... before it's too late."

"What?" Webber spat out the fragment of cigarette sticking to his lower lip, and for once he was shaken out of his usual calm. "Why? What's the matter? What's gone wrong?"

"There's been an explosion," Harold shouted. He had to shout, for spray from the bows was rattling against the wheelhouse windows like water from a hosepipe. Ordinary speech was usless. "There's been an accident in the stokehold. Sam—the stoker—he's badly scalded. He'll have to be taken to hospital at once."

Harold leaned against the wheelhouse door, his chest heaving. His legs were trembling, and he felt that if he had been asked to stand without support he would have fallen down. He waited, expecting to see Mat Webber thump urgently with his heel on the trapdoor which gave access to the chartroom below, where Mike Grory would be sleeping.

Had Mat ordered him to fight his way across the waveswept foredeck to rouse the man who acted as radio-operator, he would have done so without hesitation; but Mat did neither thing. He stared for a moment, then asked:

"Has the Chief sent you?"

"The Chief?" Harold gaped, wondering for a moment who the Chief could be.

"Chief engineer, you fool ... Bill Howson. Did he send you with that message?"

Harold gulped, then shook his head. No, the Chief had most certainly not sent him, and just for a moment he had an uneasy feeling that perhaps he had been a little too hasty. He remembered that he had kicked Bill Howson in the face, and had come up here against the man's orders. It gave him a qualm. Then he thought of Sam Pickup . . . Sam, with face and shoulders red and shiny from scalding steam and water. What the little stoker's hands had been like Harold could only guess.

"The Chief did not send me," Harold said firmly. "I came because the stoker is badly scalded, and he should be got ashore as soon as possible. Scalds are dangerous . . . especially when a man is working amongst coal dust."

Mat Webber gave him a queer look, then turned to the voice-tube which connects engine-room and wheelhouse. By means of that tube, conversations can be carried on between the man in charge above deck and the man in charge of the engine-room. Mat took a whistle out of the voice-pipe, put his mouth to the pipe and blew down it as hard as he could.

In a similar pipe in the engine-room there would be a similar whistle, and Mat's hard blow would send a shrill piping through the engine-room. The mate replaced his whistle, and waited.

A minute passed. The deckhand at the wheel was juggling with the steam steering. One moment the steering engine would be spluttering away, turning the rudder to port, then, as the *Annie* slewed under the lunge of a heavy sea, the steering engine would be busily turning the rudder to starboard. It was not an easy night for the man at the wheel.

Harold leaned against the wheelhouse door, his feet wide

apart. The wild yawing and plunging of the trawler was beginning to make him feel a little sick.

Then there was a shrill piping from the speaking-whistle. Someone in the engine-room was answering Mat's signal. Mat took out the whistle, waited a moment, then spoke into the mouthpiece:

"Mate here . . . that you, Chiefy?"

From then on for several minutes, Mat Webber listened. It was Bill Howson at the other end of the speaking tube, and Bill was explaining what had happened. Finally, Mat spoke:

"Doesn't need a doctor, eh?"

In the engine-room, Bill Howson gave a snort of disgust. "Doctor, my foot. I don't know what yarn that interfering young maniac has given you, but Sam'll be as right as rain in a few days. His hand is the worst." Then, as a sudden thought occurred to him, he said more quietly: "Listen, Mat, I'll tend Sam's burns. Send me some lint and bandages . . . y'know the sort of stuff I need . . . picric acid, tannic acid, or whatever they're using these days for scalds. They never seem to know what to stick to. Anyway, send it down . . . and send it down with that stowaway. Know what he's done to me?"

Mat cocked an eyebrow, and turned for a moment to take a swift look at Harold. He had not forgotten what had happened less than an hour after the *Annie* sailed from her home port. Harold Jackson had punched him, Mat Webber, mate of the *Blackball Annie*, on the nose. Yes, punched him on the nose and got away with it.

"What has he done?" Mike asked softly, and his voice was smooth as silk.

"Kicked me in the teeth, that's all," came the hoarse

whisper up the tube. "Yes, I've got lips like puff pastry, and two front teeth so loose they're dancin' a jig while I'm talking. I've got somethin' to say to that little . . . anyway, I'll save my breath. Send the bandages down with him. I'll do the rest."

"With the greatest pleasure," Mat assured him. "I'll send the stuff down at once. G'bye."

He pushed the whistle back into the mouth-piece, then turned to Harold and said:

"No, he doesn't need a doctor, laddie. I've got some stuff in the medicine chest that'll do fine for him. Y'know, trawler hands have got to be tough. They are tough. You sit down a minute, while I get what's necessary."

Harold breathed a little sigh of relief. He had half expected the mate to blaze up at him, but Webber seemed to be in quite a good temper.

Mat slipped down into the chartroom, and there was a muffle of voices. Mike Grory slept like a cat, and the slamming of the wheelhouse door, and Harold's shouting, had wakened him. Mat explained what had happened, then got what was necessary from the well-stocked Frst Aid box. He wrapped them in an oilskin pouch. There was lint, cotton wool, bandages and gentian violet.

"Mind you don't get them wet," Mat urged, and held open the port door while Harold backed out. Once the door was closed again, Mat began to laugh, while the deckhand, struggling with the wheel, cast wondering glances at him, and waited for an explanation. Mat gave him one. It was a joke he could not keep to himself. He told how their stowaway had kicked Bill Howson in the mouth, puffing his lips and loosening his front teeth.

"The kid's going back now like a lamb to the slaughter.

Bill's in a temper, and you know what he's like when he gets mad. I've got a kind of feeling that our high-and-mighty stowaway is going to get something what'll do him a power of good. What's more . . . there won't be anybody down there to help him. He bust me one on the nose . . . but the skipper stopped me clouting him. Hm! I wish I could be down there," and Mat winked at the deckhand, then rolled another cigarette.

The struggle along the stormy deck left Harold breathless but somehow exhilarated. He felt he had conquered something when he finally slipped into the passage leading to the engine-room ladder. Out on deck the wind was screaming, and dark walls of water were thundering along the *Annie's* flanks, throwing her this way and that, pounding her, yet failing to do any real damage. Some of the thrill of conquest was in Harold's eyes when he fought his way down the swaying ladder. It was no mean feat to cross the stormy deck twice, and still be alive and unhurt.

The thrill died away, however, when he turned to deliver the oilskin packet containing the bandages, lint and gentian violet. Sam Pickup was sitting on the engineer's locker, a half-smoked cigarette held gingerly between his slightly puffed lips. Bill Howson was standing by the steam throttle. He had fired the boiler, and the steam gauge now showed just over two hundred pounds pressure. It was Bill's mouth which made Harold forget the joy of having won his battle with the elements. The engineer's lips were badly puffed, and the lower one was split.

"Don't stand there gawping," Bill roared. "I can't leave the throttle yet. Attend to Sam's burns, if you've got the stuff."

"Yes . . . of course." Harold was suddenly very nervous. Bill looked like a man who is waiting his time; forcing himself to be patient. Harold wished he had not kicked out so violently. The engineer's lips looked an awful mess.

He turned to Sam and began to clean the burns before applying the gentian violet, and he wondered that any man could sit so still with such burns. Face, shoulders, arms, they were sullen red, scalded, but not quite to the point of blistering. The right hand, however, was badly blistered. Yet while Harold, working as gently as he could, treated the affected skin, the little stoker sat like a statue. Only when Harold was winding bandages in place did Sam lean forward and whisper:

"Listen, cully, if I was you, I'd kind of tell Bill what a blamed fool you reckon you'd been, an' how sorry you were. See what I mean? Bill ain't a bad sort . . . but nobody likes bein' kicked in the mouth."

"I still think you ought to go ashore," Harold said doggedly. "If these burns turn septic, you could be . . . . well, you could die, you know. You could. I was only going for help."

"Yes, but you kicked him in the gob," Sam said soberly. "It were a mistake, I know. You thought these here burns were more serious than they are. You can't be puttin' trawlers into port just 'cause somebody's got hurt. How'd you reckon old Josh Jackson made his money, eh? Not with spending too much time thinkin' about folks like me."

"My grandfather would have insisted on you being put ashore." Harold said stubbornly. "I know he would."

"Grandfather!" Sam said, surprise in his voice. Then, as if suddenly remembering that Harold had said his name was

Jackson, he asked: "Here . . . what did you say your name was?"

"Jackson. Harold *Jackson*, and my grandfather is Josh Jackson, owner of the Jackson Trawlers."

"You're kiddin'," Sam whispered, but it was obvious he was wondering.

"I'm not," Harold said curtly, and went on: "I've told the skipper, and I've told the mate, but they won't believe me. They will . . . later. Once I get ashore, I'll make them pay for what they're doing to me. You wait and see."

Sam stared. He had a queer feeling that this pale-faced youth was not pulling his leg at all, but telling the sober, honest truth.

"Are you tellin' the truth, matey?" he asked.

Harold nodded, busy now tying a knot in the bandage. "Why should I lie to you?"

"Aye, why should you?" Sam agreed. Then, in a confidential whisper, he said: "Listen, you'd better tell old Bill what you've just told me."

Harold sniffed disgustedly.

"Why should I? I've told the others, but they only laughed at me. I don't suppose he'd take it any other way."

"Tell him, matey, just the same," Sam pleaded. "Look, Bill's a good sort. He is really. One o' the best; but he's rare an' mad with you just now. An', listen, he did save you from a bad accident earlier on, didn't he? Why, you'd have been mashed up like a boiled tater if he hadn't stopped the engine when you fell into the sump. Saved your life, he did. Now . . . you warn him who you are."

"What good will it do?"

"Well," Sam coughed, it was an embarrassed little cough. Then he explained: "You see . . . I'd be a bit sore if you

was to kick me in the kisser . . . mouth, that is. Bill's goin
to belt the hide off you when he has a minute to spare. I:
you tell him who you are . . . it might make a difference.'

Harold looked round. Bill was still at the throttle, and
there was no friendliness in his expression. In fact he looked
as if he could hardly wait until Harold had finished his
first-aid work before coming over to take full payment for
his thick lips and loosened front teeth.

The last knot was tied. The last dab of gentian violet or
skin which needed no bandage. Harold put the first-aid
equipment together and rolled it into the oilskin pouch
Then he rose to his feet. At that Bill Howson shouted to
Sam:

"Come and stand by the throttle, Sam. I've a bit of a
job to do, and I can't wait to get going on it."

Sam sighed, looked appealingly at Harold, then went over
and stood beneath the throttle, ready to shut off steam when
the stern lifted, and open up again when the propeller was
once more in the water.

Bill very ostentatiously rolled his sleeves a little higher
revealing biceps which looked hard and powerful.

"I wouldn't do nothin' hasty, Bill, if I was you," Sam
urged. "He's got somethin' important to tell you, what
makes things look a bit different. I'd listen if I was you.'

Bill sneered, and, his clenched fists on his hips, he looked
at Harold and asked:

"Well, out with it. What've you got to say for yourself?'

Harold swallowed. He wanted to apologise to Bill, but
the engineer's truculent attitude made an apology difficult.
It would seem as if he was apologising in an effort to avoid
paying for what he had done; an attempt to get out of being
punished. Harold had never willingly knuckled under to

anyone. He had a lot of his grandfather's obstinacy and fighting spirit in his make-up. So, facing the sneering Bill, he did not apologise. Instead he snapped:

"I thought you might like to know, before it's too late, that I'm Josh Jackson's grandson. *The* Josh Jackson who owns this trawler. One day I'll be the owner . . . and don't say I didn't warn you."

Bill frowned, and his eyes narrowed. He turned to look towards Sam, who nodded eagerly, anxious that Bill should do nothing which might land him in trouble with the owner. Bill turned back to Harold.

"So you think you can kick me in the teeth, and please yourself what you do in my engine-room, simply because you are the owner's grandson, eh? Well, I'll tell you somethin', my bucko. I don't care if you are the Emperor of China, never mind Josh Jackson's grandson. There's nobody breathin' can bust my lips and loosen my teeth *and* get away with it. When the skipper sends you down here as a 'prentice stoker, that's what you are as far as I'm concerned. You're a 'prentice stoker, and you do as you are told." He unbuckled the heavy leather belt about his waist, and folded it, holding the metal buckle in his right hand.

"If you were big enough," he said quietly, "I'd make you put your fists up; but you're only a kid . . . a cheeky, hard-faced brat; so I'm going to treat you like I'd treat a cheeky brat. Bend over that locker. I'm going to teach you that, when you're aboard ship, you obey orders. As for you being the grandson of old Josh Jackson . . . even if you were, which I don't reckon you are . . . he'd approve of what I'm going to do. Now . . . bend over."

"I'm warning you," Harold said wildly. "One day I'll be owner of this ship, and . . ."

"I'm not worried about warnings," Bill said grimly. "Bend over . . . or I'll bend you over."

Harold backed as far as he could, and, when he was brought up sharp by the ship's side, he suddenly reached out and jerked a heavy adjustable spanner from its rack. The head made an ugly weapon, and, with its fourteen-inch handle, was a formidable thing to face. Harold swung it viciously, and Bill Howson backed away.

"What you are doing, m'lad," he said evenly, "is mutiny. And, if you were a prince o' the Royal blood, it wouldn't . . . look out," he suddenly yelled, and looked to Harold's right.

It was an old, well-worn trick, but Harold fell for it. He half-turned, startled by the shout. Bill lunged forward, and a second later was twisting Harold's wrist so that he had to drop the spanner, or have his wrist broken.

"You're not so smart, after all," Bill grunted, as he forced the struggling Harold round, and down, bending him over the tool locker. Then he swung the heavy leather belt. A moment later there was a resounding "thwack", and a yell of pain. Four times the strap rose and fell. Bill did not spare his muscles. He meant Harold to remember the occasion.

There was only one yell of pain. For the last three strokes, Harold only quivered a little. Then he was allowed to stand up.

Bill began to buckle on his belt again.

"When you've a bit more sense," he said calmly, "you'll thank me for this. If I'd reported this to the skipper, you'd have been in court soon after we got back home. As it is, if you promise to obey orders while you're down here, I'll forget what's happened. You're one o' the crew of this trawler, and don't you forget it. Now . . . gimme your word that you'll go into the stokehold and deputise for Sam, and, as far as I'm concerned, that'll be the end of the trouble."

It was a fair offer, for what Harold had done could have brought serious trouble when they got ashore had the matter been reported to the authorities. Harold, however, was in no mood for thinking that way. White-faced, he stood and glowered at Bill. The four strokes from the heavy leather belt had stung, and would sting for some time to come; but the greatest hurt was to his pride. He had never been thrashed like that before. When he spoke there was a quiver in his voice.

"When I get ashore," he promised, "I'll see you go to jail for what you've just done. You can't flog me, and you know it."

Bill laughed, and gave his belt a tug to pull it in to its right hole.

"That's one of the funniest things I've heard," he chuckled. "What do you reckon o' that, Sam? He says I can't flog him . . . and me just thinking I had done. Queer, isn't it?"

"You won't be laughing when we get ashore," Harold insisted. "I'll put you in court."

The smile left Bill's face.

"I'll have to wait for that," he said coldly. "In the meantime . . . are you going into that stokehold, or shall I take my belt off again? It seems like four strokes isn't enough for you. Are you going to stoke that boiler, or do you want some more?" and he made as if to unbuckle his belt again.

Without a word, Harold turned and made for the narrow passage leading through to the stokehold. It was almost six o'clock now, and there was a suggestion of greyness about the engine-room skylights. The new day was coming, cold, stormy, but it did seem as if the wind was decreasing a little; the worst of the gale was over. The *Annie* was still rolling, but she was not lifting her stern out of the water quite so often now.

In the gloom of the stokehold—Bill Howson had replaced the smashed electric light bulb—Harold could see that the finger on the pressure gauge was beginning to slip back a little from the two hundred pound mark. He picked up the shovel and groaned. If anyone had suggested twenty-four hours earlier that he would soon be stoking fires in the bowels of a north-bound trawler, he would have laughed them to scorn. But there was no laughter in his eyes now; only a sullen fury. He was learning to obey orders, and it was not pleasant. Jerking open the starboard firebox, he bent to scoop coal from the pile on the stokehold plates. The one thing which made it possible for him to keep going was the thought that his turn would come.

"Wait till I get ashore," he kept muttering. "Just wait. I'll make them wish they'd never been born. It's their turn now, the bullies, but my turn will come. They could have put me ashore easy enough, if they'd wanted. When my turn comes, they'll wish they had put me ashore. They've not downed me, not by a long chalk."

CHAPTER SEVEN

A SHOCK FOR MIKE GRORY

FOR FOUR and a half days the *Blackball Annie* plugged steadily north, then nor'-west. She reached the Pentland Firth, said to be the stormiest spot around the coast of Great Britain. From Duncansby Head to Dunnet Head, there are twelve miles of water where it is said five tides meet, and the little island of Stroma, north-west of John o' Groats, divides the swirling rip of the Atlantic rollers, sending them racing eastwards so that even a powerful trawler can be brought to a standstill if the tide is against it.

Mike Grory was lucky, for the tide was in his favour, sweeping the *Annie* westwards at seventeen knots. Then it was good-bye to the Scottish shores, and out into the blue. They caught glimpses of the Orkneys, and then there was only a vast expanse of grey seas, white topped, and without a sign of even a seabird.

Harold suffered in the stokehold. His hands were soft, and, before he had finished his second watch in the stokehold, he had to have his blisters pricked and bandaged. Bill Howson merely grunted when Harold pointed out that it was painful to use a shovel.

"You've got to toughen up, m'lad," he growled. "You get back to the fires. You'll thank me later on. When I've finished with you, you'll be able to earn your bread and butter in any stokehold. That'll be somethin,' won't it?"

Choking back the bitter words which came to his tongue, Harold stumbled through to the darkness of the stokehold.

He was learning something he had never known before . .
and that was to obey orders.

By the time they had passed the Vestmann Islands and were
steaming west along the coast of Iceland, he was beginning
to feel better. He was leaner in the face, but some of the
terrible stiffness and utter weariness of the first three days
had gone.

He had wept tears of bitter rage more than once in the
solitude of the stokehold, but had decided not to complain
again. He had been to see Mike Grory once, to report what
Bill Howson had done—flogging him with a heavy leather
belt. Mike had simply taken his pipe from between his
teeth, raised his eyebrows, smiled, then said:

"I daresay you asked for it. We're always willing to give
folks what they ask for aboard the *Annie*. Go on, and don'
be more of a cry-baby than you can help."

Once on the fishing grounds he was taken off stoking, and
made an apprentice deckhand. He watched the great trawl
"shot" over the side. Then he went to his bunk for two and
a half hours. At the end of that time, the trawl was hauled
up from the sea bed, and more than two tons of codfish
tumbled out on to the deck. They had been brought from
the fifty-fathom depth, and some of them were more than
a yard long. The gutting pounds, where the men worked,
was a foot deep in writhing fish, and Harold was supplied
with mittens and a gutting knife. By the time he had been
trying to gut cod for a couple of hours, he realised he had
never known what real weariness meant, not even in the
stokehold. The codfish swung about this way and that in
his hands. More than once he was swung off balance, and
crashed down among the slimy fish. Each time, grim-faced,
he got up again.

The crew referred to him jokingly as "His Lordship", and were ready to be friendly. They could admire courage, and they knew Harold was suffering. They wanted to be friends, but every little gesture they made was rebuffed. Harold was not going to unbend. He was saving it all up until he got ashore. Then . . . it would be his turn.

In four days of fishing, with catches heavy all the time, Harold grew dirtier and dirtier. There was no time to think of washing, or sleep. It was gut, gut, gut. Now and again the cook would call them in for a meal. Now and again he would bring great steaming jugs of scalding tea on deck, and there would be a few moments' rest while they drank . . . then back once more to the never-ending toil. Mike Grory had earned his name for being one of the toughest skippers ever to take a trawler to sea. He could find fish when no other trawler was getting any.

Had Harold been less weary, he could have enjoyed the majesty of the scene. Stately gannets sailed through the air on wings which never seemed to move. Now and again they would drop like plummets into the water, and emerge a few moments later with a small fish in their beak. They would toss it into the air, catch it by the head, and gulp it down. Whenever the trawl was brought up, there would be a screaming horde of seabirds thronging the air, waiting for food.

There was practically no night, for they were on the fringe of the Arctic Circle, and, though the northern summer was almost over, the sun was still only dropping below the horizon for an hour or so around midnight.

At the end of four days, a sudden gale put an end to fishing for the time being. The trawl was hauled inboard, stowed secure, and, when all fish on deck had been gutted, washed and put on ice, the crew were allowed to go below for a well-earned rest.

Mike Grory, though he had had as little sleep as the crew during the past four days, nevertheless took over the wheel, and, with no one else above decks, turned the bows of the *Annie* into the rising storm, and, with the engines turning over at half-speed, steeled himself for a four-hour vigil.

After an hour, he turned on the short-wave radio to relieve the monotony. He knew that at least two other Jackson trawlers had followed him north at two-day intervals, and he began to call them on the short-wave set with which all Josh Jackson's deep-sea trawlers were fitted.

"Mike Grory in the *Blackball Annie* calling *Toros* or *Yellow Star*. Are you receiving me? Over."

He made his call several times, allowing a minute interval between each, and was about to flip the switch for sending once again when a voice with a strong Welsh accent broke the relative quiet of the wheelhouse.

"Dai Evans of the *Toros*, calling Mike G. in the *Annie*. Are you receiving me, are you receiving me? Over."

Mike assured the little Welsh skipper of the *Toros* that he was "receiving him", and then flipped the switch over to reception. At once the Welshman asked a question which made Mike stiffen.

"I thought you would have been on your way back by now, man. Haven't you had the news?"

"News!" Mike said, flipping the switch to "sending", "What news? I haven't "spoken" to anyone since I came up. Been too busy. Struck a good patch of cod, and been hauling in double-bags every time. What's the news?"

"You haven't heard?" Dai Evans sounded incredulous.

"But I thought you had the new owner aboard. Josh Jackson's grandson. Isn't he with you?"

Tough skipper though he was, and hardened to the many dangers of the Icelandic fishing ground, Mike Grory's heart did a little hop, skip and jump at that. What did Dai Evans mean?

He asked for a proper explanation, and the Welshman gave it.

"You mean you didn't know old Josh was dead, man? Knocked down by a runaway milk-cart horse . . . two days ago. Duncansby Head was asked to try and get you. The new owner . . . is wanted back home immediately. You do have him aboard, Mike, don't you?"

Mike had been grinding his teeth hard on the stem of his pipe. Slowly he took the pipe out of his mouth, and soberly said:

"Yes, I've got him aboard. Are you sure old Josh is dead? I mean . . . he wasn't just badly injured."

"No, no . . . he's dead, and sorry I am to say it. A grand man he was, and a good friend to me. You always were the lucky one, Mike . . . to have the new owner aboard, eh? Sitting on velvet you'll be from now on, eh? Good friends you'll be with him, I'll bet."

"I wouldn't bet if I were you, Dai," Mike said grimly. Then, as if he was just merely sorry that old Josh was dead, he went on: "Yes, I have got the lad aboard, and I'll have to send for him and break the news. The trip has done him a power of good, Dai. They won't know him when he gets back. Anyway, I'll ring off . . . and get moving. We'll be heading for home within the hour."

He stood for a moment staring out through the wheel-house windows. Visibility was less than half a mile now.

The clouds were low, and being swept along by a steadily rising wind. The waves were short-pitched, steep, and angry. It looked as if a real snorter was blowing up.

"But nothing to the snorter that will blow up when I tell the kid that he's boss. Oh . . . tch-tch-tch-tch!" Mike shook his head. "It just would happen to me. Treat him rough, that's what old Josh said, and that's what I've done. I can just imagine what he's going to say and do when he realises that he's the new owner . . . and my boss."

Ruefully he tapped the dead ash from his pipe, then, calling the engine-room, he asked the second engineer to send the stoker up to the aft cabin to waken Mat Webber, and order that man to come to the wheelhouse.

Slipping a holdfast over the kicking wheel, he slowly refilled his pipe.

"The trouble is," he murmured, "if I start trying to explain to Mr. Harold Jackson, that I was only obeying the orders of his grandfather, it'll look as if I'm whining. Josh . . . I don't know whether you are in heaven, or the other place, but you've landed me in an awkward spot . . . a darned awkward spot."

Mat came hurrying to the wheelhouse, sleepy-eyed, and wondering what had gone wrong. Mike had told him he could have four hours in his bunk. He had been below only a few minutes over an hour.

"Somethin' wrong, Mike?" he asked, as he slammed the wheelhouse door to shut out the blustering wind and the driving spray.

"Before I tell you, Mat . . . bring Bill Howson here," Mike said. "I think he ought to know as well. It's nothing concerning your folks, or Bill's . . . I haven't picked up a B.B.C. S O S, or anything like that."

"Thank goodness for that," Mat growled, and sped off into the the wind and spray again.

Five minutes later he was back, and with him the chief engineer. They had brought three pint mugs of scalding hot tea.

"That's a good idea," Mike said, taking one of the pots. "I need a stimulant . . . and I reckon you lads will, too. I've just had a message from the *Toros*."

"Dai Evans?"

"Yes. He tells me that old Josh is dead."

There were exclamations of amazement and sorrow, from both Mat and Bill. Genuine sorrow, too. Josh they knew as a hard-driving owner, but a good man, just, and straight as a die.

"Aye, that news is bad enough," Mike said, "but this is worse. We've got the new owner aboard."

"Oh, lor!" Mat Webber slopped tea down his jacket, and gulped. Bill Howson merely stared, and said:

"New owner?"

"How did you treat your apprentice stoker, Bill?" Mike asked, a touch of sardonic humour in his voice.

"Treat the little brat," Bill growled, "I belted his backside with my leather. He'll not forget Bill Howson in a hurry, I'll tell you. I've worked him till the sweat's poured down his face. I told him I'd learn him to kick my teeth loose, and . . ." Then Bill stopped, and a look of dismay spread over his face. He had suddenly remembered that Harold had tried to persuade him that he was the owner's grandson. Bill sucked in a mouthful of tea, then asked: "Is he . . . the new owner?"

"I'm afraid he is."

"Well . . . strike a light," Bill groaned, "and me calling

him all the names under the sun for being a lazy good-for-nothing. I told him he wouldn't forget me . . . and, by gosh, he had the cheek to tell me he wouldn't.'"

"And he won't," Mat Webber growled. Then a wry grin chased the gloom from his face as he said: "Well, what do you know, eh? If we'd tried to get ourselves in the wrong with him we couldn't have worked harder. But . . . who the heck would have thought old Josh would go and get killed. We're sunk. Mike . . . what are we going to do?"

Mike struck a match and sucked at his pipe for a moment. Then he said:

"There's only one thing I'm going to do. I'm going to take my medicine. I'm not crawling to a whipper-snapper like him. I'll tell him I ordered you two to haze him . . . that'll put you in the right. Now, Mat . . . go and waken him. He's sleeping in the fo'c'sle like any ordinary ship's hand. Lor . . . but he's going to crow when he gets the news. He's been praying for a chance to get his own back . . . and by gosh his chance has come!"

Bill Howson returned to his bunk in the aft cabin. Mat braved the spray-lashed foredeck, and disappeared into the fo'c'sle.

Mike stared into space. All his life as a trawlerman he had been with the Jackson trawlers. Several times he had refused tempting offers from other firms. Now, if he was any judge, his time as a skipper with the firm was drawing to a close. Harold Jackson had sworn to be revenged, and as the new owner of the Jackson trawlers he would have absolute power to do as he liked. If he wanted to discharge Mike Grory, no one could stop him.

A few minutes later, Mat Webber climbed into the wheelhouse, sucking a cigarette which was limp with salt water. Harold Jackson followed him a minute later.

"You wanted me?" he asked, and there was a sulky note in his voice. He was dog-tired; tired and muscle-weary. But one thing he had learned in the nine days he had been aboard the *Annie*, and that was to obey orders.

"Yes, I wanted you . . . Mr. Jackson," Mike said slowly, and cupped his hands about his pipe bowl as he tried to light the new tobacco there.

Harold looked up, amazement in his eyes. "Mr. Jackson!" Mike really had said that, and sudden excitement blazed in his eyes. It could mean only one thing. A message had come through from his grandfather.

"So you've heard from my grandfather, have you?" he demanded, his voice charged with satisfaction. "You know, now, who I am."

Mike nodded soberly.

"Yes, I'm afraid we do. We haven't heard from your grandfather, Mr. Jackson. I only wish we had."

"What do you mean?" The excitement was washed out of Harold's eyes. He had a sudden premonition that there was bad news coming.

Mike broke the news as gently as he could, and the colour drained from Harold's face. Slowly his shoulders sagged, and he turned very wearily to lean his elbows on the ledge which ran round the wheelhouse just below the windows. He stared across the tumbling welter of broken water, but saw none of it. Mike puffed at his pipe. Mat Webber slowly rolled a cigarette, then a second. He put this on the window ledge by Harold's elbow, but it was not seen.

For ten minutes no word was spoken in that tiny wheelhouse. The wind was whining through unseen crevices.

Water was being whipped over the plunging bows and splattered noisily against the wheelhouse window. Occasionally the steering engine clanked a little as Mike kept the *Annie's* bows into the storm.

Then, from the chartroom below, came a thin, high-pitched whistle. Harold did not look round, but the whistle had an immediate effect on both Mike and his mate. Mat took the wheel and Mike tumbled below as quickly as he could. Mat Webber blew sharply into the voice-tube connecting wheelhouse with engine-room and, when he was answered, he said curtly:

"Stand by. Get a full head of steam . . . we've just had a whistle on the emergency signal in the chartroom. It might be an S O S."

Silence again; but outside, the thin funnel of the *Annie* began to belch smoke. The stoker was piling fuel on his fires, building them up so that if it was an emergency, he would have a full head of steam.

There was a faint mutter of words from the chartroom. By means of the radio-telephone, Mike was speaking to someone, and it was the person who had sent out the special signal which rings the alarm on modern sea-going radio sets, to announce that an S O S message is about to come over the air.

Mike Grory came up to the wheelhouse, his face set. With a flip of his big hand, he pushed the engine-room telegraph indicator over from " Half speed ahead " to " Full speed ahead ". There was an answering ring from below and within seconds the vibration of the floorboards in the cabin increased. The triple-expansion engines were under wide-open throttle, and the *Annie* began to buck as she slowly built up to her full speed. Now she was taking it green over the bows, and miniature avalanches of water poured off the whaleback and chased in creamy torrents along the midships to the stern.

Harold did not seem to notice anything. He was slowly recovering from the terrible shock of learning that his beloved grandfather was dead. His thoughts were not on the *Annie*, they were a thousand miles south, where the man who had meant everything to him was no longer alive, alert, a master of men and ships. Josh Jackson was dead.

Suddenly Harold turned and faced Mike.

"We're going home," he said. "Home as fast as you can take me. I want to get back for the funeral. When did it happen? I've got to get back. They won't bury him before I get back. I know they won't."

Mike shook his head. His face wore a heavy frown.

"I'm sorry, Mr. Jackson," he said gently. "We can't go back . . . yet. There's a French trawler in trouble. Just had an S O S from her. She's about thirty miles nor'-west of here, and we happen to be the nearest ship."

Harold stared at him, then some of the colour came back to his face, some of the old haughtiness returned to his voice as he snapped.

"We are going back, Mr. Grory. I've got to get back, and I'm ordering you to turn round."

"I'm sorry . . ." Mike began, and was interrupted.

Eyes blazing, Harold snapped:

"I think you are forgetting something, Captain Grory, aren't you? *I* am now the owner of this trawler. And *I* am ordering you to return to port . . . at full speed."

CHAPTER EIGHT

A SKIPPER IS SACKED

SLOWLY Mike Grory tapped the tobacco from his big curved pipe. He stared for a moment or so at the new owner of the *Blackball Annie*, then he said quietly:

"Since you came aboard this trawler, Mr. Jackson, you've learned a lot of things you never knew before. You've learned that deckhands, stokers, and even mates, have to work, and work hard for their bread and butter. You've learned a lot about the sea . . . and I think it has done you good. There's one thing more you've got to learn, or you'll never understand the sea . . ."

"Cut out the sermon," Harold said impatiently. "I've given you an order, and I'm now the owner of this trawler."

Mike went on as if he had not been interrupted.

"This thing you've still got to learn is that no ship's master ever refuses to answer a call for help. No, not if he's master of the biggest liner in the world, or the smallest fishing smack floating. It's a law of the sea."

"I don't care what it is," was Harold's retort. "I want to get home . . . and this is my ship. I'm ordering you to . . ."

"There are men's lives at stake," Mike said gently. "Isn't that important?"

"Of course it is, but there must be other ships about, and they could answer this S O S, couldn't they?"

"They can, and they will," Mike assured him. "We are going because we happen to be nearer than anybody else. We can be there first."

"I see," Harold sneered. "And if you do the rescuing, you get a medal, eh?"

For a moment it looked as if Mike was going to slap Harold's face; but, with a great effort, he held himself in check, and said quietly:

"Round these coasts an hour can make all the difference between saving lives and being too late. That's why we are going, as fast as the engines can push us along. I've seen a ship smashed to rusty plates in an hour . . . and if *we* were on the rocks I'd want everybody to come as fast as they could. Look at those seas, Mr. Jackson. Would you like to be swimming just now? Will you take the responsibility of leaving men to take their chance on somebody else getting to them in time?"

For a moment Harold hesitated. Then, stung by the contempt in Mike's voice, he snapped:

"Yes, I will. I'll take full responsibility for anything that happpens. I'm the owner, and I want to get home quickly. If there's any trouble, you can say that I ordered you to steam for home."

Mike shook his head.

"What you are saying doesn't let me out, Mr. Jackson. I'm master of this trawler. Understand that . . . I am the master, and the skipper of the French trawler *Jean* has asked me to help him. He hasn't asked the owner of the *Blackball Annie*. He's asked me, Mike Grory, and I'm skipper. And that's your answer."

Had he not been so upset over the news of his grandfather's death, and had he not been so weary from his four days' work in the gutting pounds, Harold would have agreed that Mike Grory was doing the right thing; but he was in a bitter mood. He had lost the one man he loved more than anyone else in the world, and it seemed as if Mike Grory was just being awkward.

Eyes blazing with anger he said:

"Very well, if you won't obey orders, I'll have to find someone who will. You've had your warning. If you won't take the ship home at once, I'll get someone else to do it."

Mike struck a match and sucked at his pipe before saying:

"You carry on, Mr. Jackson. As you say . . . you are the new owner, and this is your ship. Go ahead."

Harold turned to the silent Webber.

"Could you take command?" he asked.

Mat Webber shot a swift glance towards Mike, then nodded.

"I've had a sea-going master's ticket for the past five years, Mr. Jackson. Only been waiting for a chance to show what I could do. Your grandfather promised me a trawler the first chance that came along."

"Good," Harold smiled triumphantly, then turned to Mike and said crisply: "Mr. Grory, you are discharged. From now on, Mr. Webber is in command."

Mike took out his pipe, gave Harold a long look of disgust, turned and stared at Mat Webber, then spat out:

"Do you mean you're going to take over, Mat?" he asked, and it was obvious he did not believe Webber would do such a thing. Mat, however, nodded.

"I'm going to do just that, Mike," he said firmly. "I've waited a long time for a trawler of my own, and Mr. Jackson can rest assured I'll have him back in Hull just as soon as possible."

"You see, you're not indispensable, Mr. Grory," Harold pointed out, and to Mat: "I shan't forget this, Mr. Webber."

"I don't suppose you will," Mat chuckled, "and once

've got this French trawler out of trouble, we'll head for
home faster than smoke."

Mike Grory looked up; the savage frown melted from
his face, and he grinned.

The look of triumph vanished from Harold's countenance.
"What did you say?" he demanded angrily. "You are
to head for Hull at once. That's why I have made you
kipper."

Mat shook his head, and there was no twinkle in his eyes
when he answered:

"Not on your sweet life, Mr. Jackson. And if you'll stop
giving orders for a minute, I'll tell you something. I've
seen your sort before, and I'm going to tell you . . ."

"Mat," Mike Grory interjected. "I wouldn't say too
much if I were you."

"For once, Mike, I'm going to have my say," Mat said
fiercely. "This little squirt is too chockful of his own
importance to know the difference between chalk and cheese.
Well, I'm going to try and tell him something what'll do
him good. Listen, Mr. Cock-a-hoop Jackson. If you were
to offer me a thousand quid right now, I wouldn't take
Mike Grory's place. D'you hear? Not for a thousand quid,
I wouldn't. You can't *buy* loyalty! Money doesn't buy
everything, m'lad. That's a lesson you'd better learn now.
I've sailed with Skipper Mike Grory for fifteen years . . . and
you think I'd throw him over just for the chance of taking
his place, you poor little fool. Why, if we struck a rock
now, you'd be the first to start yelling for help. You'd
want every ship within a thousand miles to come hurrying
to save your rotten little skin. And if anybody passed you
by, you'd never stop yelping about their cold-blooded-
ness."

"It isn't that at all," Harold said peevishly. "I want to get home to attend my grandfather's funeral."

"And you'd let mebbe a score of men and boys die jus for that, would you?" Mat went on savagely. "Well, fo once you can't have your own way. The skippers in th trawling business don't wear gold-braided cheese-cutters Mr. Jackson. They don't go about wearin' natty blu uniforms and brass buttons, but there are as many honest to-goodness seamen in trawlers as you'll find anywhere i the seven seas. You made me a skipper a minute back. Wel I've been skipper of the *Blackball Annie*, and now I resign And when we get back to Hull, you'll be able to fire m proper. But there's one thing you do know . . . and that' what I think about you. You're too darn mean to giv anybody the right time. You wouldn't do that if you' watches in every pocket." Then, turning to Mike Grory he lifted his hand in a mocking kind of salute as he said "Mat Webber returning to duty as *mate*."

Harold was white-faced and fuming, and when Mik said: "I'm afraid there's no one else capable of takin command, Mr. Jackson," Harold stamped out of the wheel house. He fought his way across the well-deck, getting we to the waist by the time he reached the fo'c'sle. A fev minutes later, however, he returned, and now he wa carrying a small bundle of crumpled clothing, his sport jacket, his blue poplin shirt, his canary yellow pullover, an his salt-stained brown shoes. He stood for a moment looking at Mike Grory and the mate, then he said quietly

"You can move your things out of the chartroom a soon as you like, Mr. Grory. As owner of the *Blackba Annie*, I intend to have a little more comfort for the re mainder of the trip."

Mat moved across and lifted the trapdoor which gave access to the chartroom below.

"Allow me, *sir*," he said sarcastically.

Just as sarcastically, Harold said:

"Thank you, Mr. Mate."

After the trapdoor had been dropped into place, there was a silence in the wheelhouse for a couple of minutes. Then Mat said:

"Well, Mike, I reckon me and you will be looking for a new ship once we gets back home."

Mike nodded, then said:

"Go and warn the crew, Mat. I don't know how long it will take us to get to the *Jean*, but they'd better have a meal and get into their oilskins. I've a feeling we've a sticky bit of work in front of us."

"Aye-aye." Mate and skipper looked at each other for a moment, then nodded, and for the time being Harold Jackson was forgotten.

For four hours the *Blackball Annie* punched her way through rising seas. Like all trawlers, she was buoyant as a duck, rising under the waves whenever possible; but she took a lot of heavy seas aboard even at that. The storm had reached almost hurricane strength, and practically every vessel in the vicinity had run for the shelter of the nearest fjord. If that was not possible, then they were facing into the storm, with just enough way to keep them there. Only one or two vessels had picked up the *Jean's* S O S message and were struggling grimly on, trying, against terrible odds, to reach the stranded Frenchman.

There were times when the *Annie* was brought to a complete stop, as wave after wave smashed down in a

flooding torrent of yeasty foam over her whaleback, holding
her bows down and keeping her screw out of water. Down
below, Bill Howson had taken over, and was saying un
printable things as he had constantly to shut off steam
to avoid letting the engines race to ruin when the propeller
came out of the water.

At times even the hard-bitten Mike Grory wondered i
he was riding his luck too hard. One giant green wall o
water curled over the starboard bow and made the trawle
shudder as tons of water smashed on to her deck. The
heavy planks, which were dividing the fore-deck into
"pounds," were torn loose, swept along and over the por
side, after smashing with sledge hammer blows agains
the wall of the chartroom. That moment brought Harold
Jackson hurrying up into the wheelhouse, his face pale.

"I shall hold you responsible for any damage," he said
sourly, when Mike assured him that everything was al
right. "I don't think the weather is fit to go on."

"We're not far from where the *Jean* went ashore," Mike
said quietly. "Do you want us to stop now? She's ashore
on one of the worst spots round the coast of Iceland."

After a moment Harold asked:

"Well, what can we do, if the lifeboat hasn't been able
to get the crew off?" He turned and glared at Mat Webber
as the mate gave a grunt of disgust before saying:

"It's about time you started learnin' something, m'lad
Did you say 'lifeboat'? You're not sailing round the coast
o' Britain now, you know. Lifeboat. Cor, lumme!" and
he turned in disgust to stare ahead, trying to peer through
the sheeting spray smashing continuously over the whale
back, so that it splattered on the plate glass windows o
the wheelhouse with the sound of spent shot.

"There are no lifeboats round this part of the coast,"
Mike explained. "For one thing there are precious few
ports, and only the odd fishing hamlet here and there. As
the mate said, you're in a different kind of world up here,
Mr. Jackson. You're more or less on the fringe of civilisation.
A few hundred miles north of here and you come to the
ice-pack. You left a lot of safe and comfortable things behind
when you left Hull."

He might have said more, but at that moment, the old
cook stumbled into the wheelhouse. He was soaked to the
waist, and gasping for breath. By a string about his neck
he carried several pint mugs. In his right hand a big enamel
jug filled with coffee. This he handed to Mat Webber.

"Thought you'd mebbe like a drink," he said, addressing
Mike Grory. "I've made some sandwiches for you and the
brats . . . and I'm trying to get some broth and other stuff
ready, just in case. Is that all right?"

"Good man," was all that Mike Grory said, and the cook
went out again to fight his way back to his galley.

Harold was given a mug of coffee, and for a minute or
so he had the strange feeling that these trawlermen were
not the same breed of men seen ashore. No one had asked
the cook to prepare food for the men they were out to
rescue. No one had asked him to fight his way across waveswept decks to bring the coffee to the men in the wheelhouse.
The cook was an old man; but he had made sandwiches,
coffee . . . and he had risked his life to bring the jug and the
mugs to the wheelhouse.

Harold sipped his coffee, and about ten minutes later the
wheelhouse door opened again. Once more the cook came
in. He was carrying sandwiches, and he asked for lint and
a bandage. As he entered his galley, a savage lurch of the

Annie had threatened to throw his big pan of broth on to the floor. He saved the pan, but a slop of scalding broth had blistered his arm.

While Mat Webber was painting the blister with gentian violet, Harold noticed that the cook was not wearing sea-boots. His feet were shod in a pair of cracked and broken shoes. Harold was dry-footed and comfortable. The cook, old, weary, ill-shod, had made two trips to the wheel-house, and was now ready to go back and battle with his cooking pots so that, if they did rescue anyone from the French trawler *Jean*, there would be hot food for them. He got no extra pay for it. There was no "danger money" for risking the flooded deck. It was just part of the job, and Harold was suddenly rather ashamed of himself.

There had been no grumbling from the tired deckhands when they had been roused, and told to get ready in case they were wanted for a rescue job. The only person aboard the *Annie* who had groused, and even tried to stop the rescue attempt, had been her owner, Harold Jackson.

He finished his coffee, and looked at Mike Grory and Mat Webber. They were both staring out to the north, both intent on catching the first sight of the stranded trawler. A minute or so later, when Harold had almost made up his mind to ask Mike Grory's pardon for the hard and stupid things he had said earlier, a red light pierced the gloom over to starboard. Mike Grory was already ringing down to the engine-room "Stand by engines", when the look-out, perched on top of the wheelhouse, was yelling out the news.

The *Annie* was turned shorewards, and, as he stared across the tumbling welter of savage waves, grey and wicked-looking, Harold was afraid. The *Jean*, faintly seen through clouds of bursting spray, lay on a rocky ledge some eighty yards or so from the foot of a towering cliff. Every few moments a great rolling wall of water would surge in from the sea, it would pass over the *Jean*, flinging spray so high as to completely hide the vessel. Each time it seemed as if the trawler had been blotted out for ever.

After watching half a dozen such waves, Harold turned away. He felt sick. It seemed impossible for any vessel to stand such a buffeting, and not break up. He had read of rescues often enough, but he had never quite understood what they involved. Newspapers printed headlines, "Heroic Rescue", and such words, but, though he came of trawling stock, Harold had never been brought face to face with the real thing before.

It did not seem possible that anything could be done. If the *Blackball Annie* went in too close, then she would suffer the same fate as the *Jean*. Cruel rocks would tear at her plates. She would be aground, and would stay there, pounded by successive waves until she broke up.

He looked at Mike Grory. The skipper of the *Annie* had taken the wheel.

"What can you do?" Harold asked, a plaintive note in his voice. "You can't go in close enough to help, can you?"

Mike did not answer. He was staring ahead, intent, oblivious to anything but the tricky task of taking the *Blackball Annie* as close inshore as possible.

"Half," he said, and at once Mat Webber whipped the handle of the engine-room telegraph over to "Half speed ahead". Then back to "Stand by engines".

The black bulk of the towering cliffs seemed to stretch right up to the sky. The air was filled with flying spray, and the roar of waves pounding the base of the cliffs made the air tremble. It was a chaos of noise, frightening to anyone but an experienced seaman. Harold felt cold in the pit of his stomach. He wanted to stop Mike Grory taking the trawler any farther into danger. He felt that any moment, now, they would feel a shuddering jar as the trawler ground on to the reef of rocks which had trapped the *Jean*.

Nearer, nearer, the trawler seeming to feel her way through the great crested waves which surged shorewards. Then Mike gave a shout:

"Astern . . . quick!"

Harold closed his eyes, and waited. He heard the clash of bells as the watchful Bill Howson in the engine-room answered the signal. He felt the quickening vibration of the floor as the propeller raced for a moment in reverse before gripping water once more, and he waited for the jarring crash as they went on the reef.

CHAPTER NINE

A RESCUE ATTEMPT FAILS

THERE was no jarring crash. Only the sudden gust of cold wet wind as the wheelhouse door was opened and closed again. Harold opened his eyes. He was sick with fear, and looked wildly at Mat Webber when he saw that Mike Grory had left the wheelhouse.

"Where's he gone?" he shouted. He had to shout, for the thunder of breaking waves made ordinary conversation out of the question. "Why has he left us?"

Mat, his hands on the brass-bound steering wheel, looked round, as if surprised to see Harold there.

"He's going to try and get a line across . . . a rocket line," Mat shouted, then turned and stared ahead. He was slowly bringing the *Annie* round, so that her stern was towards the cliffs. It was a ticklish manœuvre. If they should be caught by a couple of the huge waves, broadside on, it would easily mean their being swept in too close.

Mat had a part-smoked, unlit cigarette dangling from his lips, but he seemed quite calm.

Slowly the *Annie* came round, rolling violently, so that Harold had to brace his feet, and cling desperately to the edge of wood in the port corner of the wheelhouse. Then they were round, and Mat allowed the trawler to drift a little closer inshore before whipping the telegraph handle over to "Slow ahead".

Harold made his way gingerly on to the deck. The crew

were lined up, watching the unlucky *Jean*, while Mike
Grory fixed his rocket gun to the rail, and the third hand
adjusted the coils of light line which were to be carried over
to the *Jean*.

Mike looked round for a moment, noticed Harold, and
said grimly:

"There's a lifebelt in the chartroom. Go and get it on.
It's under the mattress. I don't want you drowned."

Harold stiffened, and for a moment his hate of the skipper
increased, until he saw that every other member of the
crew on deck was already wearing a lifebelt.

After a momentary hesitation, he returned to the wheel
house, descended to the chartroom, and found the lifebelt.
It looked as if it had never been worn, and it took him
several minutes to put it on correctly.

When he went on deck again, he was startled to discover
that they seemed to have drifted even closer to the cliffs.
They were less than a hundred yards from the stranded
Jean, and the crashing roar of breaking waves was ever
louder.

On deck again, with water two feet deep washing past
him, he watched the final preparations for the attempted
rescue. The crew were assembling a breeches buoy. A stouter
line had been made fast to the thin line Mike was to fire
across to the *Jean*.

When all was ready, Mike squeezed the trigger. There was
a puff of smoke which seemed to shoot high into the air
as if it would go right to the top of the cliffs, and the coiled
line snaked out like lightning.

Harold screwed up his eyes, watching the progress of the
rocket. It had been well aimed, and seemed certain to fall
right across the *Jean*. Then a gust of wind must have

caught it as it started to fall. The smoke veered. Harold bit his lower lip, then closed his eyes as a chorus of curses and groans from the deckhands confirmed what he had feared. The rocket had been blown to one side, missing the *Jean* by a few yards.

For a minute or so everyone stood and waited, hoping that they might have been mistaken, that the line had really crossed the *Jean*, and would be hauled in.

Nothing happened. The stranded trawler seemed completely without life, and very reluctantly the rocket line was hauled back again, then coiled carefully in its box, while Mike loaded another rocket.

For two hours after that first shot, they made attempt after attempt to get a line across, while in the wheelhouse Mat Webber fought with all the skill at his command to keep the *Blackball Annie* from being rolled too close inshore. The engine-room telegraph bells were clashing every minute or so.

Time after time the sodden rocket line was hauled back and re-coiled. Time after time the thin plume of smoke swept into the air, curved, seemed about to drop athwart the *Jean*, only to be whisked this way or that by the capricious currents of air sweeping off the glistening wall of rocks behind.

The old cook brought sandwiches and coffee. Harold took a sandwich thankfully. It was almost two inches thick and had a half-inch layer of corned beef between the two pieces of bread. The coffee was scalding hot, strong, syrupy sweet with sugar, but it put new life in them all.

Harold needed something like that. He was wearing oilskins, a sou'-wester, and sea-boots; but water had somehow seeped down his collar, and the cold wetness had spread across his shoulders. Miserable and cold though he was, he had been unable to tear himself away from the trawler's stern rail. For the first time in his life he was in real danger; but he stood there, forgetful of it. Now he was thinking only of the Frenchmen aboard that poor, battered *Jean*. It was impossible for them to stay on deck, for each wave which swept shorewards exploded over their stern like a bomb, throwing water high and wide. He felt he had some idea of what they were enduring. They knew that a trawler had come to their rescue, yet each passing minute made their rescue less certain.

The continuous pounding of the waves was grinding the keel of their craft harder and harder on the rocks. The finest steel plates in the world, the best forged rivets men can make, will not stand up to that sort of thing for ever. Even while they had been there, the crew of the *Annie* had seen the Frenchman's funnel smashed over the side. They had seen his stumpy stern-mast crumple, and tossed into the raging seas.

When the last rocket had been fired, and the sodden line hauled back, there was a long and solemn silence. Mike Grory unscrewed his rocket gun from the rail, pursed his lips, and then, without a word, turned to the wheelhouse.

No one spoke, though every man on deck watched and waited. They had complete faith in their black-jowled skipper. If there was anything to be done, Mike Grory would do it. He was not the man to leave seamen in distress.

Faintly through the chaos of sound came the jangle of bells, and everyone waited. What was going to happen now? Was Mike going to put the *Annie* even closer inshore? Even the toughest deckhand quailed a little at the thought. They had been flirting with death for a couple of hours already. To go nearer the *Jean* was asking for trouble.

Instead of going nearer, however, the *Annie* began to surge forward, heading once more for deeper, and safer, waters. She was under full speed, and within two minutes the *Jean* was lost to sight.

Then one of the deckhands, a thin, lanky individual, spat morosely over the side and shook his head.

"That's not like the ' bloke '," he shouted. "We can't just leave 'em. We should try a boat. For cryin' out loud, what's he up to? We're not runnin' away now. Who'd risk a boat? We could get a line to her by boat."

Two or three hands went up immediately. Others of the crew stared shorewards for a few moments, as if weighing the chances a small boat would have in such seas, then two more hands went up.

The deckhand who had made the suggestion began to explain what they ought to do, but all the time the *Annie* was fighting her way farther and farther away from the shore, until the black and glistening bulk of the towering cliffs were shadowy, and difficult to see.

Harold had a lump in his throat. It did not seem possible that they were now running away from the men on the *Jean*. Back there, where the waves were exploding into mountainous walls of spray, a ship was slowly dying. Dying, and with her a whole crew of helpless men.

He turned to the wheelhouse. The crew of the *Annie* could only grumble among themselves. They were deckhands, and must obey every order. *They* were not allowed to argue with the skipper, but with Harold it was different. He wouldn't let Mike Grory abandon the *Jean*.

Forgotten now was his bitter and angry denunciation of the skipper and mate, when they had insisted on trying this rescue. He had insisted then that some other vessel should answer the Frenchman's distress signal. Now he had been face to face with the horror of a shipwreck. He had seen those rockets fly out so bravely, time after time, and had seen the power of the wind turn them this way and that, like some malignant devil, determined not to let the Frenchmen be rescued.

If old Josh Jackson had been alive at that moment, he would have nodded his head in content, for here was the real Jackson breed come to life in Harold. This was not the pampered youth who had been shanghaied aboard the *Blackball Annie*; this was the grandson of old Josh, and the son of the father who had died while battling his way with a convoy through the Mediterranean, while the sky was black with Nazi dive-bombers.

Storming into the wheelhouse, Harold looked angrily at Mike, who was trying vainly to light his pipe.

"What's the idea?" he shouted. "You can't just leave them like this. There may be a score of men aboard the *Jean*. What do you think you are doing? Do something. You can't just run away and leave them."

Mike looked at him over his cupped hands. Then, in a very calm voice, he asked:

"All right. You're the owner. What can we do? I've just been trying to contact the *Toros*, to see how far away they are. I've no more rockets."

Harold swallowed hard, then said:

"The crew are willing to take a line across by boat. They're certain they can do it. It's a chance, and I insist that we take it. You can't leave the crew of the *Jean* to die."

Mike's eyes hardened.

"I see. The crew are willing to take a boat, are they? And you think it's a good idea."

"It's much better than steaming away, isn't it? At least we could try."

Mike nodded.

"I had thought of it," he admitted, "but it's dangerous, very dangerous."

"We just can't leave the Frenchmen without trying something," Harold insisted.

"All right," Mike agreed, "and I suppose you are willing to take an oar? It's a fifty-fifty chance that anyone who tries to take a line across by boat will not come back. Now, what do you say? It's easy enough to agree to the crew having a go. Will you go with them?"

CHAPTER TEN

THE SPIRIT OF OLD JOSH

FOR A MOMENT, Harold merely stood and stared at Mike Grory, and there was a grim, cynical smile on the trawler skipper's face as he said:

"That's different, isn't it? It sounds a good proposition to send a boat across to the Frenchman, so long as other people are taking the risks. Let the deckhands go, and drown if the boat is capsized; but it's a different kettle of fish if there's danger for you." Then, in a sharper voice: "Well, can't you answer? I asked if you were willing to take an oar?"

Harold's cheeks slowly reddened under Grory's biting sarcasm. He faced the older man, looking him straight in the eyes. Then he said simply:

"I didn't think I'd have been good enough. I can row, but rowing in a sea like this isn't the same as rowing on a river."

"Well, I suppose any excuse is better than none," Grory said bitterly. "Anyway, I oughtn't to blame you. You don't belong to the world of real people. You are more for tennis, and motoring, and, I suppose, picnicking on the river in a punt."

He made for the wheelhouse door, but Harold grabbed him by the coat sleeve, and forcibly halted him. Mike swung round, his other hand lifted as if he meant to knock the detaining hand away; but the blow did not fall, for Harold was saying:

"Listen, Mr. Grory. You daren't have said things like that either to Grandfather or my own father, and you shan't say them to me. I'm a Jackson . . . as much as they ever were, and I'm going in that boat." With that he stalked past Mike Grory and clattered down the wheelhouse ladder to the deck.

Mike looked at his mate, and Mat Webber's bushy eyebrows lifted.

"He's got guts, Mike; you've got to admit that."

Mike shrugged, then hurried out on to the deck. By this time the *Blackball Annie* had completed a half-circle, and was steaming back towards the dark blur of the coastline. The crew of the trawler were in a bunch, huddled against the driving spray, and taking no heed of the water which swirled past them knee-deep, every time the bows lifted a great flood on to the deck.

"I've been in touch with the *Toros*," Mike shouted, "and Dai Evans is coming as fast as he can; but he won't be here for hours, yet. He shipped a big sea which tore his winches loose."

There was a chorus of exclamations of amazement at this news. The great double winches set before the chart-room of the trawlers are firmly bolted down . . . bolted down firmly enough to take the terrific strain of a trawl towing along the sea bed perhaps a third of a mile, or more, behind the ship. Any sea which could rip those winches loose must have been a terrific one indeed. No wonder Dai Evans would be late. His ship, the *Toros*, must have taken a hammering.

"I was hoping he might have been near enough to have got a rocket line over to the *Jean*," Mike went on. "I don't think the wind's as bad as it was. However, Dai's miles

away, and the Frenchman is beginning to break up. You
know what that means."

Heads nodded. Anyone thrown into the water near such
a rocky coast would be lucky to get ashore alive.

"What about trying a boat?" someone demanded.

Mike nodded.

"I've thought of it," he admitted, "and if there had been
any other way, I wouldn't do it. But, there isn't any other
way. It means a boat . . . or standing by and watching them
drown."

"Ah, now you're talking," the tall, thin deckhand
named Wally Small, shouted. "Put me down for a port
oar."

"Any others?" Mike asked, and the crew to a man lifted
their hands.

Mat Webber, leaving a deckhand at the wheel, had come
to Mike's elbow, and he muttered:

"Put me in, Mike . . . I'll take Wally and George. They'll
do me fine."

"Get the boat off the chocks," Mike ordered. "Two of
you get a drum of lubricating oil off Bill in the engine-
room. You'll need all the smooth water you can get."

The idea that they were not going to desert the stranded
Jean had an amazing effect on the crew. They had been
sullen, angry, and muttering among themselves; but now
there was the prospect of action, they changed in a flash.
While two raced for the engine-room to bring up the
drum of oil, the others scrambled on top of the cook's galley
where the ship's boat was lashed on chocks.

Mike turned to Harold.

"Well," he asked coldly, "still willing to take an oar,
or were you just bragging?"

"I'm going with the boat," Harold said. He was scared, or he could not get out of his minds' eye the violent explosion of spray at the stern of the *Jean* every time a wave rolled up to her. How any small boat could get to the stranded Frenchman without being stove-in he could not imagine; but . . . he meant to go. Mike Grory had challenged his courage, and there was a lot of old Josh Jackson in Harold. He had plenty of guts.

"All right, you shall go," Mike agreed. "Get to the galley and tell Cookie to give you a square meal. You'll need more than a sandwich under your belt for this job. We might get a line across, but I doubt if we'll get our boat back again."

Harold nodded and turned away, not sure whether Grory was trying to frighten him, or merely telling the truth. He stared towards the land, and decided Grory was only telling the simple truth. A boat might reach the *Jean*, but if it got back again, it would be something like a miracle.

In the aft cabin, the cook was cutting bread and buttering it as fast as he could. Seated at the table were Mat Webber, Wally and George. George was a great hulking brute of a man, who said little, but was enormously strong. He had shoulders like an ox. Wally was thin, tall and wiry, but Harold thought he could probably make up to George's colossal strength by sheer skill at the oar. What Mat Webber could do, Harold had no idea, but he fancied the burly mate must have had plenty of small boat experience. They made a redoubtable trio.

As Harold sat down, George gave him a broken-toothed grin, then reached for a sandwich and engulfed it in one bite.

"Do you want some grub?" the cook asked, and it struc
Harold that these men did not realise that he was going wit
them. He wanted to tell them, so that he could be include
in the half-whispered conversation going on between then
They were talking about some previous rescue attempt c
a similar nature, when one man had been drowned.

"What happens if . . . if . . . well, suppose someone doe
get drowned this afternoon?" Harold asked.

"Here, turn it up," Wally grunted, reaching for anothe
sandwich. "Why should anybody get drownded? No sens
talking like that. In any case, I were measured for a new su
'fore I come away this time. Paid two quid deposit on i
too. I'm not losin' that, matey; betcha life I'm not," an
he laughed. Mat Webber laughed; George laughed; an
Harold felt awkward. He badly wanted them to know h
was going to share the risk with them, yet baulked at tellin
them here, in case they thought he was merely boasting.

Half-way through the hurried meal, he had an idea, and
leaving the aft cabin, went down into the engine-roon
He borrowed a stub of pencil from the harassed Bill How
son, and a sheet of paper. He wrote busily for severa
minutes, then fled for the deck as he heard someone yel.

"Come on, you guzzling divils. We're about right fc
the boat."

Reaching the deck, Harold was in time to see Mat Webbe
go nimbly over the stern, and into the boat, bobbing at th
end of a short painter. A drum of oil was held suspende
over the stern of the trawler, and from a small hole, punche
in the bottom, oil dripped out. It spread into the thinnes
possible film over the angry waves, and had an amazin
effect. It soothed the yeasty walls of water, and provided
relatively smooth path from the *Annie* to the poor *Jean*.

It was no easy task getting into the small boat, and two deckhands were working hard to keep the boat from being stove-in against the stern of the trawler while George and Wally waited their chance to get aboard without capsizing her.

Finally they were aboard, and Harold stepped up; but at that moment Mat Webber yelled:

"Right, lads . . . let her go." The painter was slipped, and the three men bent to their oars, while behind them trailed the life-line which was to connect rescue ship to ship in distress.

"Wait!" Harold yelled, and might have dived overboard had not Mike Grory grabbed him by the arm and jerked him back.

"Take it easy," Mike said. "I never intended you to go. It needs men with experience for a job like this."

Harold stumbled away from the stern where the deckhands were assembled, and he felt as if someone had slapped him full in the face. Scared of going in that small boat, he had somehow managed to screw up his courage for the attempt, and all the time Mike Grory had never intended to let him try. He realised, dully, that the skipper of the *Annie* had merely been testing him to see what courage he possessed.

From the waist of the trawler, he watched the ship's boat moving slowly but surely towards the *Jean*. It seemed crazy to imagine that any small boat could get there in one piece, yet the three men at the oars had a skill and cunning which seemed equal to the task.

Mat Webber was standing in the stern, sculling gently with an oar, keeping the small boat just right for each wave which rolled up behind them. Wally and George were pulling as calmly as if they were merely out for a pleasure jaunt on some smooth-watered lake.

One moment they would be in full view, poised on the crest of one of the big waves racing shorewards; then they would be down in the trough, completely hidden from sight. Each time they vanished like that, Harold's heart threatened to skip a beat.

Among the deckhands at the stern of the *Annie* there was no talking. Two of them were paying out the line, the others watched that little boat. Many of the deckies were sucking at unlit, spray-dampened cigarettes. They were not given to silly flights of imagination, but one and all knew that if there was an Angel of Death, then that angel was beating his wings over those grey waves. One slip on the part of Mat Webber, or his two companions, and the boat would be engulfed. It needed only one small error of judgment.

When disaster did overtake the small boat, it was due to no error of judgment, but one of those little things which happen so quickly that there is no time to prevent an accident. The rope, which was being paid out so carefully, had been coiled in a box. Then, just when it should have come out smooth and straight, a loop came up and kinked.

The deckhand watching the loops bent to straighten the rope, and as he did so the *Annie* shipped a big sea at her waist. A screaming flood two feet high washed towards the stern. The kink in the rope flopped to one side, and must have been directed by the goddess of ill-luck, for it looped itself over the end of a projection clamped to the bulwark. There was no time to free it. Mat Webber and his men were straining at their oars. They were nearing the French trawler, and as they strained so they tightened the rope. The loop clamped like a vice about the projection.

The accident was over in the space of twenty seconds. The rope tightened until it was like an iron bar. The small boat, now some eighty yards distant, was beginning to rise to the top of a giant wave. Then the rope attached to the stern tightened, pulled the boat back, and down.

Instead of rising buoyantly over the wave, the boat was held, water spilled over the stern. The wave swept on, and the boat was tipped up, her bows rising in the air as if a giant hand was pushing underneath.

Mat, Wally and George were tossed in a tumbling heap on top of one another, and disappeared in the water. The boat, half-filled, was carried shorewards by the wave. The rope tightened, tightened, and then snapped.

The break occurred about twenty feet from the stern of the *Annie*, just as Mike Grory was bending his great strength to try and free it.

Like a viciously swung stock-whip, the broken end of the rope whipped back, singing as it came. It struck Mike on the head, and must have laid his scalp open to the bone had he not been wearing a sou'-wester. The sou'-wester took the vicious crack, but it could not break the full force of that blow. Mike was sent face down, hitting his forehead on the iron top of the ship's bulwark.

From there he slid sideways, to sprawl full length in the water flushing the deck. He lay there, limp, unconscious, while the deckhands stared in horror. A moment or so before, it had seemed as if victory was within their grasp, as if they might rescue the French trawlermen. Now they had lost three men and their only boat.

CHAPTER ELEVEN

NEW OWNER TAKES COMMAND

HAROLD was unaware of the accident to Mike Grory. The sudden disaster which had overtaken the small boat kept him with his gaze riveted on the stern of the *Jean*. Why the small boat had suddenly up-ended, to throw the three trawlermen into the water, he did not know. What he was sickeningly aware of was the fact that blinding spray hid the stern of the French trawler and three of the *Annie's* crew had vanished.

The spray cleared, and for a moment or so he could see the overturned boat careering towards the shore. Then it must have struck something, for it shot into the air, and its planking was split apart. Harold shivered. If that could happen to a clinker-built dory, what must be the fate of the three men?

He screwed up his eyes at a sudden movement at the stern of the *Jean*. Two of the Frenchmen had come out of the ship's galley, hoping to lend a hand. They must have been watching the approach of the Britishers, and had been waiting for the right moment to lend a hand. Now they were leaning over the stern, and to Harold's joy, he saw two black dots break surface. The Frenchmen leaned over, a hand was stretched up to them, then once more a wave broke over the trawler, and flying spray hid everything from sight.

Harold groaned. It seemed impossible that any man

could take such a blow and live. Yet, when the spray had
subsided again, one man was being hauled over the stern;
one man out of three, for the other black dot in the water
had vanished.

Another wave hid the stern, and, when the spray from
that had gone, Harold yelled with joy. He could see two
heads. One very low in the water, as if the man was being
held up by his comrade. Who it was he could not tell, but
the Frenchmen were already feverishly throwing a looped
rope.

For several minutes after that, wave after wave broke
over the stern of the *Jean*, but each time, when the spray
had gone, the two men were still there, a little nearer
safety. Harold was glued to the rail, hardly daring to
blink, in case something dreadful should happen while his
eyes were momentarily closed.

The Frenchmen, brave to the point of foolhardiness, kept
at their posts in the stern, and eventually hauled inboard
a limp figure. Two waves later, the third survivor was
hauled aboard.

"They've got all three . . . they've got all . . ." Harold
had turned to where he expected to see the deckhands of
the *Annie* standing, but there was no one in sight. The men
had lifted Mike Grory, and he was no featherweight, and
had carried him gently down to the aft cabin.

Hurrying aft, Harold saw the last man going through
the trapdoor into the cabin, and he followed, almost stepping
on to a deckhand who was about to go to the wheelhouse
for the First Aid box.

"I'll go!" Harold turned and fought his way to the wheelhouse. Entering, he was in time to see the third hand push
the engine-room telegraph over to "Full speed ahead", a

signal which was answered almost immediately by Bill Howson at the controls below.

"What's that for?" Harold demanded, feeling the increased vibrations underfoot as the trawler's engines were put on to full speed.

"What are you talkin' about?" the third hand snapped. He was anxious, and suddenly afraid of the responsibility which had been thrust on him. He had seen the deckhands carry Mike Grory below, and realised that, with Mat Webber away, he was in charge.

"What am I talking about?" Harold echoed the third hand's words in sudden fury. "Haven't you seen what's happened? The small boat smashed, and our men dragged aboard the *Jean*. Where are you taking us?"

"Out to deep water," was the gruff retort, "and you get out of here. I've no time for back chat. Go on, get out."

Harold opened the trapdoor and dropped down into the chartroom. He grabbed the First Aid kit and fought his way back to the aft cabin. Mike Grory had been laid on one of the lockers which served as seats at meal times. He had a nasty bruise right in the middle of his forehead, and both his eyes were swollen. He was beginning to make little moaning sounds, but it was obvious that, even if he became conscious within the next few minutes, an hour or possibly more would elapse before he would be fit to take charge of the trawler again.

The deckhands were arguing as to what was best to do now that they had no boat. They were talking of trying to float a line down to the *Jean*, but Harold did not stay to listen. He went up and then down into the engine-room. Bill Howson was standing by his controls, his face as black as thunder.

"What's happenin' up topsides?" he demanded angrily. "Here I am, and nobody thinks to let me know what's going on. Where are we going? Has he . . ."

"Listen," Harold snapped, and gave Bill a quick explanation of what had happened. Bill's eyes went bleak. Mike Grory out of action! Mat Webber and two deckies marooned with the Frenchmen aboard the *Jean*! It was a nightmare situation, and, wide though Bill's experience had been, he did not know what could be done now.

Harold, however, had decided what was to be done.

"Listen to me," he said decisively. "You know I am Harold Jackson . . . and the new owner, don't you?"

"Yes," Bill nodded agreement.

"Then, let that fool in the wheelhouse know, will you?" Harold asked. "He's taking us out to sea . . . and I'm not having it. He's got to take us back. We can't leave the *Jean*, can we?"

Bill sucked at his lips for a moment before asking:

"What can we do? We've lost our small boat. We've lost Mat . . . and he's had more experience of this sort of work than any man breathin'! Short of swimming across, don't . . ."

Harold stopped him. Eyes suddenly brightening, "That's it," he shouted. "Swimming . . . of course. I could get a line to them."

"Don't be a fool," Bill growled. "You couldn't get a line to them. Why you'd be . . ."

"You listen to me," Harold was transformed now. He was a leader, decisive, direct, knowing what to do and how to do it. "I may be a lousy stoker, and I may be little good at gutting codfish, but I'm one of the best swimmers in the north of England. I'm going to swim over to the *Jean*.

Now, you call the chap in the wheelhouse and tell him who I am."

Bill Howson stared at Harold for a moment, then shook his head.

"Now, it's no use talking like that, Mr. Jackson," he said soothingly. "I don't know who's in the wheelhouse, probably the third hand. If he's reckoning on taking us out into deeper water, then . . ."

"Will you answer me one question?" Harold asked coldly.

"What?"

"Am I the owner of this trawler? You heard Mike Grory say that my grandfather was dead. I *am* the owner of this trawler, and as long as Mr. Grory isn't able to command, and as long as the mate isn't here . . . then I'm going to have my way."

Bill scratched at his thinning hair.

"The point is this . . ." he began hesitantly.

"The point is that there's a trawler on the rocks," Harold shouted angrily. "She may be breaking up at this minute. Mat Webber is there, and the two deckhands . . . as well as the French trawler's hands. Do you want them all to die?"

Bill turned abruptly and went to the speaking-tube. He was there for a minute or so, then he came back.

"I've told him," he said. "He'll do what you want."

"Good. Now, listen, I gave you a sheet of paper a few minutes ago. Have you got it?"

Bill produced the hurriedly-written note. He looked at Harold questioningly.

"I want you to sign it," was the request, in a very quiet voice. "It's a . . . a sort of will, in case anything happens.

to me. Read it, sign it, and if I don't come back . . . be sure it goes to Grandfather Jackson's solicitor. He'll know what to do."

Before Bill had time to smooth out the paper, Harold was gone. He looked down into the aft cabin, and Mike Grory was slowly regaining consciousness. Startled faces were turned upwards as Harold shouted down.

"I want some of you on deck. I'm going to take a line over to the *Jean*. I'm going to swim it over."

He allowed the trapdoor to drop, then fought his way against the wind and rain to the wheelhouse. He stared at the third hand for a moment, then asked:

"You know who I am?"

"Yes . . . Mr. Jackson," the third hand agreed. "Chiefy told me."

"Right. Head the trawler back towards the *Jean*, and get her where she was earlier. I'm going to take a line over . . . I'm going to swim."

"Swim?" The third hand gasped at the idea.

"Don't start arguing," Harold snapped. "If I'm the owner, then I'm going to have my own way. You do as you are told . . . or there'll be trouble."

He felt exuberant as he slid down the wheelhouse ladder again. It was like playing a fierce game of football, and knowing that though your opponents were good, you were even better, and sure to win. He felt nothing *could* go wrong now.

Several deckhands had already come up from the aft cabin, and word had obviously gone around that "His Lordship", as they had jokingly nicknamed Harold, was old Josh Jackson's grandson, and in consequence was now the new owner.

They were preparing a rope, but one of them warned Harold.

"Listen, cully . . . er, Mr. Jackson, I hope you know what you are doing? You wouldn't get me to swim across to that trawler now if she were filled with pound notes. You'll never make it."

"If we don't do something," was Harold's reply, "our men, as well as the Frenchmen, will die."

The deckhands looked at one another, and nodded. That was true enough. There *was* only one chance for the men on the *Jean*, and that was by swimming a line to them.

Somebody suggested Harold stripped and was coated with engine grease. He went below and stripped down to trunks. Bill brought out a can of grease and smeared him thickly from head to foot.

When he had finished, he held out his right hand.

"Listen, laddie," he said seriously. "I've read that paper, and I've signed it. I don't know whether it's legal or not, but I've changed my mind about you. I thought you were a no-good little . . . well, never mind. I'd like to shake you by the mitt. It takes guts to offer to swim in northern water, 'specially when there's a storm blowin' . . . but anybody who can write what you've written is a . . ." He had opened the paper, and was staring at it. When he looked up, Harold had gone.

He called to the stoker to stand by the engine controls for a minute, and went up on deck. He was just in time to see Harold Jackson dive off the stern of the *Annie* and disappear into the crest of a shoreward-racing wave.

He stood for a few moments watching. He saw the head break water. He saw the grease-coated arms begin to strike out in a powerful trudgeon stroke, the line connecting the swimmer to the ship snaking out thin and dark. Then he turned to the deckhands.

"Listen, lads," he said, "I know you've pulled his leg. You've had your bit of fun with him, calling him ' Your Lordship ', and all that. Well . . . listen to this. He wrote this out a few minutes back, an' give it me to sign." Bill cleared his throat and began to read:

"' I, Harold Jackson, heir to the estate of my grandfather, Joseph Jackson, being about to attempt to go across to the French trawler, *Jean*, stranded on a reef on the coast of Iceland, do hereby authorise the family solicitors, Messrs. Huntley, Beardsmore, and Mowbray, to pay to the relatives of any member of the crew of the trawler *Blackball Annie*, who may lose his life in this rescue attempt, the sum of £500 over and above what the courts may decide is fit and proper."

"' *Signed:* HAROLD JACKSON.
"' *Witness:* WILLIAM HOWSON, Engineer.'"

"Cor," somebody muttered. "He wrote that; and me been thinkin' of him as a little stinker who . . ."

"Strewth," somebody yelled, making everybody turn sharply. "He's gone . . . he's gone under."

Harold had gone under. He had struck out bravely enough through the oil-filmed path which lay between the *Annie* and the *Jean*. He could hear nothing save the roar of turbulent waters, and could only see the *Jean* whenever a passing wave lifted him high. He felt the drag of the rope about his waist, and knew he could have made the swim far better without it.

He covered perhaps twenty yards, then a following wave

caught him as he was deciding to turn over and swim on his back. It seemed to tower over him for a moment, then crash down with devasting power on to him. It drove the breath from his lungs, it bore him swiftly beneath the surface, and, instead of seeing the leaden sky, he now saw millions of air bubbles through a quickly darkening mass of water.

For a moment he panicked, and almost opened his mouth to scream. Then the line about his waist checked him, and the very feel of it gave him sudden new courage. He turned like an otter, and began to struggle to the surface, holding his breath though his lungs were torturing him.

The rope about his waist seemed to be tightening, almost as if the men aboard the *Annie* were trying to haul him back again. It seemed as if he would never reach the surface, and when he finally came to air he was almost spent.

He did not hear the yells of encouragement from the *Annie*. He lay for a moment, paddling feebly to keep himself afloat, and sucked in life-giving air.

When he finally turned over, and began to stroke more gently in the direction of the *Jean*, he was amazed to discover that he was already two-thirds way to his objective. The current, which had set the French trawler ashore, had helped him considerably.

His delight was quickly tempered by fear. If the current should carry him quickly against the *Jean*, he might not live to climb aboard.

Beginning to paddle against the pull of the current, he turned over again, this time lying with his feet toward the shore, and it was the right move. Now, as each successive wave lifted him, he got a glimpse of the *Jean*, and could gauge his progress. There were two men in the Frenchman' tern, waiting, braving each successive flood of water which broke over them, and waiting to help Harold aboard.

Three waves bore him onwards, and then he was deposited in the trough of one directly beneath the stern of the *Jean*, and let down so low that to his amazement his feet touched rock. Above him he could see the strained faces of the two Frenchmen. One man was throwing a rope, while the other yelled a warning. Another wave was coming.

Harold made no attempt to grab the looped rope which swept down to him. At that moment he was thinking swifter, and more coolly than ever before. He knew he had one chance of survival. He must press against the rusty plates of the *Jean* before the next wave smashed him against the metal. It was his only chance.

He moved forward, and a second later daylight was blotted out as a wave swept up to the *Jean* and exploded in a torrent of hissing spume and foam.

Harold had filled his lungs, but even so he was breathless by the time the wave had gone. It seemed devilish in its power, crashing against him with the solidity of concrete. He felt bruised from head to foot, and clung there, water racing past him, clutching him, trying to drag him shorewards to his death.

Then, just as quickly, the water was gone. Once again he was in the trough between two waves, and if he did not get out now he might never get out. No one could stand more than one or two such poundings.

Again the looped rope was flung down to him. This time he grabbed, looped it under his arms, and a moment later was jerked upwards.

He did not feel the harsh biting pain as skin was scraped from his knees and shins against the rough plating of the

stern. He was vaguely aware of being in a race, a race agains
death. Breasting the winning tape in this race meant getting
over the stern before the next wave pounded him.

The two Frenchmen, worn and wearied though they were
somehow found strength to jerk him up and over. He wa
just sliding into their arms when the next wave burst ove
the stern.

Nothing human could withstand the force of the wave
and the three were flung away from the stern, and brough
up with a crash against the *Jean's* galley wall. Harold wa
incapable of helping himself, but the two Frenchmen clung
to him like limpets. The flood of water racing along the
decks tore at them, pulled them this way and that, then
was gone.

One thing filled Harold's thoughts. As he had been
hauled over the stern, he had felt a terrific jerk at his waist
then the tautness had gone, and he had a sick feeling that
the rope he had fought so hard to bring over from the
Blackball Annie had parted.

The Frenchmen helped him to his feet. They hustled him
into the galley and slammed the door just in time to preven
the next wave from flooding in.

The older man embraced Harold, and began to pour ou
an excited torrent of words, congratulating him on hi
courage, his swimming powers.

Harold shook his head, then looked down. The rope from
his waist trailed to the door. It was slack enough . . . bu
whether it went from the other side of the door across tha
heaving chaos of water to the *Blackball Annie* he did no
know. He just felt that it did not. Somewhere in that eighty
yards which separated the two trawlers, the rope had parted

He began to explain his fears. The Frenchmen, waiting

eir chance, opened the door, and once again the three
ood on the exposed stern.

In between waves, they hauled on the rope. It came in
sily, too easily, Harold thought. Yard after yard, yard
ter yard, practically no strain on it. It could mean only
1e thing . . . the last chance of rescue had failed, and, in
ying to help, Harold had merely thrown away his own
fe.

CHAPTER TWELVE

ABOARD THE "JEAN"

As HAROLD watched, there came a moment he would neve[r] forget. Over the stern came a knot. The light line he ha[d] ferried across from the *Annie* had kept intact, and here wa[s] the stouter hawser, a manila line strong enough to carr[y] a bo'sun's chair; strong enough to carry men to safety.

Making the manila line secure, the Frenchmen almos[t] carried Harold into the galley, and down to the aft cabin[.] The entire crew of the French trawler was there, we[t] shivering, and with practically a foot of water sloshing abou[t] their feet. A single oil lamp cast a miserable yellow glo[w] over the company, which included Mat Webber, George lying on the table, his eyes closed and a bandage about hi[s] shoulder. On the far side was Wally, nursing a crudely bandaged arm.

While the Frenchmen were excitedly acclaiming the new[s] that this young Britisher had got a rope over to them, Ma[t] Webber was staring at Harold, his eyes frankly unbelieving Finally he said:

"You!"

For Harold it was a moment too wonderful to describ[e] He felt ridiculously proud; proud to think he had don[e] something this stocky, powerful mate had never imagine[d] he could do. Mat turned to Wally, who was sucking a dam[p] cigarette.

"Here, Wally . . . look who's here. His Lordship!"

Wally nodded. His face was white and strained. What had happened to him, Harold did not know, but it was obvious the deckhand was in great pain. Suddenly, however, the grey face broke into a grin, and Wally said:

"Well, bust me! They said somebody was tryin' to swim across, an' I were tryin' to think who it could be. I never put your name in the hat. No. I'd have bet a thousand quid to this wet fag that you wouldn't have tried it. 'Course, old Josh were allus an awkward cuss, an' if you are his grandson, I suppose that explains it. Josh would ha' done a thing like that."

Harold knew a fiercer pride then, and the biting pain from his skinned knees and shins were forgotten for the moment when Mat Webber suddenly held out his hand, saying:

"I can't say I've much time for owners, whether they're sons or grandsons. An' I'll tell you again, you're a stuck-up young monkey, needin' a good belting. I dessay you'll fire me quick enough when we gets home . . . but, just the same, I'd like to shake your mitt. If I'd a hat on, I'd take it off to you. You're a man . . . a full-size man."

"Thanks." Harold did manage a queer sort of smile, but only with difficulty. Mat was shaking him by the hand, and Mat's grip was just about crushing Harold's knuckles together. That handshake hurt.

The stronger members of the *Jean's* crew were sent up on deck to arrange the rescue apparatus. Those who remained below were chattering away, talking about this pale-faced youngster who had suddenly given them a chance of life. He did not look like a trawlerman, but he had somehow swum through eighty yards of raging seas, and now they were in contact with the *Annie*. There was admiration and gratitude in their eyes as they looked across at him.

It took twenty minutes before the life-line was completed and the breeches-buoy had been hauled across, ready for the first man to try his luck. All through that time the *Jean* had been quivering to the steady punch of waves pounding against her stern, grinding her broken keel plates on the rocks, and straining even more the rivets which held her plates together.

The skipper of the *Jean* came down to announce that they had tested the life-line. One of their members had been safely hauled across to the *Annie*. Now the Britishers must go. It was only right that they should get back to their ship . . . they had already risked much.

George, still white-faced and limp, was carried up on deck. He went through the waves, sometimes above the water, sometimes hidden for a moment by a towering comber; but he did reach safety.

By this time Harold had been fitted out with some oddments of clothing, and when the call came for the next Britisher, Mat nodded to Harold.

"You're next," he said, but Harold merely shook his head. "Wally should go," he said.

Wally went, and then the Frenchmen who were suffering from exposure and minor injuries. Mat Webber, who was almost himself again, refused to go while there was an injured man aboard the *Jean*. Harold, feeling more of a man than ever before, also refused to go.

"I'm a good swimmer," he insisted, "and if anything went wrong, I would have a better chance than most."

Two hours slid by, for it took perhaps seven or eight minutes for each operation. The light was going now, and a feeling of acute anxiety was spreading among those left. There was no doubt about it, the *Jean*, having stood hours of continual pounding, was now beginning to break up. Her keel had long ago been ground and pounded to ruin. Now she was beginning to break in two.

Waiting in that stuffy little aft cabin, Harold found himself thinking of bus queues back home. During the rush hour, people pushed, and were rude to one another; as if having to wait for the next bus was a terrible tragedy. Here, in this poky little cabin, with death staring them in the face, the remaining members of the *Jean's* crew, patient, weary, waited without the least sign of wanting to take anyone's turn.

There were only five of them left aboard the French trawler when she suddenly canted over. She had been quivering for some time. Then, there was a shudder which could be felt everywhere; it was as if some vital part of her had finally snapped. When the next wave hit her stern, she lifted as usual, but when she settled again, as the wave raced shorewards, she had taken on a dangerous cant.

In the cabin, Mat and Harold, and the one Frenchman with them, looked anxiously towards the trapdoor, wondering for a moment if they were going to have to make a frantic fight for the open air. However, nothing happened for a minute or so. And Mat, who had been sucking at the back of his right hand, off which the skin had been badly scraped, looked across at Harold and said quietly:

"You know, you should have gone earlier, lad. I've got a feeling as you may have left it too late. It weren't right as you should have stayed. You've done your whack."

Harold merely looked and shrugged. There did not seem anything to say to that. Then there was a fumbling at the trapdoor. Mat, Harold and the remaining Frenchman, looked up, waiting for the beckoning finger which would summon one of them to go up on deck, to be taken to safety.

The trapdoor lifted, and after a moment the sodden figure of the French skipper came into view. Harold noticed that one of his sea-boots was split from the toe to the ankle, and water was squelching out.

Although the roar of the storm still made the cabin a place of ferment, it seemed as if an uncanny quiet descended on the cabin when the mate of the French trawler followed his skipper into the cabin. The two men sat down. Their faces were grey with strain and fatigue. Their eyes were red-rimmed and tired. No one spoke.

Finally the French skipper put his hand into an inner pocket. He brought out a flat tin. Opening it, he showed seven cigarettes, and he held out the tin to Harold, who shook his head, then to Mat. In that wet cabin the cigarettes were probably the only dry things.

"You weel smoke a cigarette, M'sieur," he suggested, and after a moment's pause, as if some explanation was necessary: "A . . . a last cigarette."

"So it's like that, is it?" Mat asked, reaching forward and taking one of the "smokes". "What happened?"

The tired skipper of the *Jean* held out the case to his own mate, at the same time giving a weary little shrug.

"Even a rope cannot stand everything, M'sieur. The life-line is broken. Sixteen rescued . . . five . . . " He spread his hands in an expressive gesture, and, as if to give added weight to the simple words, the *Jean* suddenly began to move.

Lifted from her resting-place by a larger-than-usual wave, she slid forward, while from beneath the cabin came the ear-splitting shriek of metal being torn and twisted against savage fangs of rock.

Slowly, but surely, the trawler began to heel over to port.

All five in that little cabin were thrown against the port wall, and a flood of water poured over them, forcing its way in via the trapdoor. The trawler was trembling violently as her keel plates were ground to ribbed steel, or torn into strips, ground and wrenched at by the irresistible force of the seas pounding at her.

The smoking lantern was swinging wildly on its gimbals, and giving just sufficient light to show the cabin floor now at an angle of forty-five degrees, and the angle growing slowly steeper.

Somehow, Mat Webber got to Harold's side. By sheer brute strength he pushed him across to the ladder. Pushed him there, and pushed him up.

"Get up . . . quick!" he shouted. "Push the trap open . . . quick; quick, before it's too late."

His fingers hooking like claws on to the woodwork, and with Mat pushing him from below, he was able to throw up the trapdoor and scramble through.

Lying in the alleyway above the cabin, he held out his hands to help Mat up. It would have been impossible for anyone to get out unaided, with the cabin at the angle it was.

Water was pouring over Harold, and into the cabin, and it was obvious the *Jean* could not last much longer. When all five were free of the cabin, they clawed their way on to the sloping deck. In the growing dusk the sight was awe-inspiring, and terrible in its threat.

The *Jean* had broken her back. Her forepart, from the bridge onwards, was canting so much that her whaleback was under water. She was leaning to port so badly that to

scramble towards the midships the five men had to wal
partly on the deck and partly on the side wall of the engine
room coaming.

"What we'll have to do," Mat shouted, "is to rope ourselve
together. We've all got lifebelts, haven't we?" He looke
at the others. One Frenchman had no lifebelt, and, withou
a second's hesitation, Mat unstrapped his belt and fastene
it on the other man. Then he saw that Harold had no lifebel
and swore an ear-blistering oath.

"Why'd you come here without a lifebelt?" he roare
"It's fools like you what make men like me . . . oh, wel
it doesn't matter," he said more gently, seeing the miser
in Harold's face. "If it's your time, you'll die, wheth
you've a lifebelt or not."

It was not a very comforting thought, but Harold scarcel
noticed. Ahead of them was the gap in the *Jean's* decl
a yawning break some five feet across, and in the darkne:
of the hold, the waters were racing noisily, washing gutte
fish about, and lumps of ice.

"Now, follow me," Mat ordered. He had taken comman
and without hesitation he scuttled past the bridge and leap
across the gap in the deck, losing his foothold on th
other side and shooting forward into a foot or more o
water.

Harold hesitated, two of the Frenchmen hesitated.
five-foot jump was not enough to frighten any man, ordii
arily; but this jump was not an ordinary one. To dro
into that seething mass of water, fish, and ice in the hol
could mean death, for where the trawler had broken i
two, jagged pieces of metalwork stuck out.

The French skipper said something sharply to his mei
One ran and jumped. He just made it, and was jerked

safety by Mat Webber. The other, a deckhand, hesitated. He was exhausted from long hours of wet and cold.

The French skipper screamed at him, but the man held back.

"Come on," Harold grabbed the man by the right hand, indicating they should run together. They did. They jumped, but the Frenchman was tired, woefully tired. He slipped as he was jumping, and his right foot missed the foredeck completely. Harold had got across, but the Frenchman, beginning to fall, was pulling him into the break as well.

Even had he wanted he could not have let the man go, for the Frenchman's grip on his hand was the grip of a terrified man.

Mat Webber leapt forward, but it was his weight against the weight of two. They hung there, poised over the gap and it seemed to Harold as if they were acrobats doing a precarious balancing act. Then, very slowly, the scales were turned against them. Mat Webber's weight and strength were not enough. They were going down backwards, and nothing they could do would stop them.

The deckhand was screaming. Then, forgotten by them all for the moment, the mate of the French trawler grabbed Mat and pulled. A moment later they were all sprawling on the foredeck. The skipper of the *Jean* came over the slowly widening gap a few seconds later, and all five stood together, breathing heavily.

Mat produced a knife, and, with the others lending a hand, he cut several lengths of rope from one of the stowed trawls. One after the other, he knotted each man to his neighbour, leaving a length of rope between each of about six or seven feet. Mat was giving commands, and the

French skipper, who spoke a little English, was translating for his two countrymen.

"We'll go over the bows," Mat said crisply. "We've drifted closer inshore since she broke her back, and I reckon with a bit o' luck we'll manage it all right. Take your time when we're in the water . . . there's no need to panic. We can't sink . . . three lifebelts between five of us should keep us up easy enough."

He wiped his mouth with the back of his hand, then added:

"We'll have a minute to get our breath back, and, while we're doing that, anybody what knows any prayers had better say 'em. We'll need all the help we can get."

He said it simply, meaning every word, and Harold looked at him, wondering how he could have imagined this broad-shouldered Britisher was a bully. To Harold, just then he seemed little short of a guardian angel. He knew what to do and how to do it. He gave out hope and confidence, talking as if they were sure to reach the shore . . . given a little luck. Harold's hopes rose. Although the situation was more than desperate, it seemed impossible to imagine that, within the next five minutes, they might all be battered into unconsciousness, and probably drowned.

Mat turned to Harold just before giving the signal that they must start. There was a grim little smile on his rugged face as he said:

"We'd orders to show you the rough side of trawlin', Mr. Jackson. Them were your grandfather's orders. Knock some of the conceit out of him, that's what he said. Well, we tried, but I'll tell you this, lad . . . we never reckoned on it being as tough as this. You'll have somethin' to talk about when you get home. That reminds me . . . if I don't

get back, tell my missus 'Good-bye' for me, will you?"
He winked, but Harold could not wink back. There was
a choking lump in his throat. It needed more than ordinary
courage to talk like that when death might be waiting for
them in the next minute or so.

Sloshing through the water which was swirling over the
whaleback, Mat led the way in the desperate attempt to
get ashore. It was a case of all jumping together, and when
they were ready, knee-deep in icy water, the mate of the
Annie gave the word.

"Over we go," he roared, "and God help us!"

They shook hands, then leapt into the raging sea. Some
sixty yards ahead of them was a towering wall of cliffs.
There might be a strip of beach there, if they were lucky
enough to get so far. If there was no strip of beach, then
they would be smashed against the glistening black cliff . . .
and that would be the end.

CHAPTER THIRTEEN

RACE AGAINST THE TIDE

WHAT HAPPENED in the next few minutes, Harold Jackson could not really remember. Sometimes he felt he was being choked by the rope about his middle, as the men tied to him were pulled different ways, sometimes he seemed to be in a huddle of bodies. All the time there was a frothing fury of water boiling about him. He seemed to have swallowed gallons, acrid and salty so that he wanted to be sick.

Then, when his head was reeling, and he had no idea where he was, or what was happening, his feet hit sand. The shock seemed to clear his head immediately. A moment later he was flung forward by a wave, and sprawled in a foot of water on a rising bank of shingle. He scraped an inch of skin from his nose, but did not feel the pain of it.

Sheer instinct to live made him get to his knees and begin to crawl upwards. There was a tug at his waist. Someone was slightly ahead of him, and striving desperately to get out of the way of the next wave. Someone was behind him, and making no effort at all.

Then Mat Webber was by his side, swearing, encouraging, tugging at his rope . . . and bringing the last Frenchman, who was completely out, away from the engulfing clutches of the undertow.

Hardly aware of what was happening, Harold reached a spot against the cliffs where only spray hit him. The sea was not reaching them. It was almost dark now, but even in the gloom he could see the battalions of waves marching in towards them, each white-topped, each breaking in a thunderous roar at the foot of the shingle beach.

He turned to Mat Webber.

"We've . . . done it," he panted. "We're saved. Do you hear . . . we're saved."

"I can hear," Mat roared back, "but this isn't the time for pattin' ourselves on the back. Let's get these ropes cut and see what's happened. Two of these poor Frenchies are out . . . mebbe dead."

"Dead!" It was a sobering thought, and some of Harold's elation vanished. He stood quiet while Mat slashed through the rope at his waist. Then he went with the mate to look at the two silent Frenchmen. They were not dead, but, during that journey shorewards, they had been injured; possibly had struck a fang of rock.

"Know anything of artificial respiration?" Mat asked, and when Harold nodded, he went on: "All right. You take him. I'll do this one. The other chap isn't fit for anything. Done up, he is."

Harold knelt by the side of the skipper of the *Jean*, and laying the man face down, he did instinctively all the things he had been taught regarding resuscitation of the apparently drowned. He felt in the mouth to see if there might be seaweed there. Then he turned the skipper's face to the side, and began artificial respiration. He pressed down on the lower ribs to drive all air out of the lungs, doing it to the count of three, then took off his weight and counted five, allowing the lungs to expand and take in air.

It was hard work, and went on and on, mechanically. Harold's arms began to feel leaden. He was conscious of a tiredness such as he had never known before. Then, quite suddenly, he was face down on the gravel.

How long he had been there he did not know. Sheer exhaustion had caused him to collapse; but it was Mat Webber who hauled him into a sitting position, and there was triumph in Mat's voice as he said:

"I'll see you gets a medal for this, cully . . . he's breathin' again. And anybody what tells me the age of miracles is past is a liar. Five of us have come through *that*." Mat waved a hand to the boiling seas. "Five of us, mind you, and all living. All we've got to do now is to get out of here."

"Are we safe, then?" Harold asked.

Mat, who seemed impervious to fatigue, looked at Harold for a moment, then asked:

"Can you climb?"

"Climb?" Harold was slow to decide what Mat meant. "I have climbed. Mountain-climbing! I've done rock-climbing."

"Ah," there was satisfaction in Mat's voice at that. "Now, that's summat like. Rock-climbing. That's what we need. You've got to get up these cliffs, and bring help."

Harold turned his face upwards, to stare into the darkness. The black wall of cliff seemed to soar to the sky.

"It's not so high," Mat said, "but you've got to get up. Y'see, it's low tide now. And we've got to be away from here before high tide . . . or we're done for. This here strip o' shingle will be under water at high tide. Get me? Under water. That's why you've got to go for help."

Shakily, Harold got to his feet, and moving back a foot or so felt at the rock. It was wet from spray, and felt smooth as glass.

"But . . . nobody could climb up here," he protested. "Not in the dark. You need to see where you're going. You might need ropes, and . . . "

"Rubbish," Mat stopped him. "If you can climb twenty
eet or so, you'll be all right. I'd go myself, but I'm a
Hopalong Cassidy. Twisted my ankle a bit . . . and whoever
oes for help has got to be able to run."

Harold was silent. He was remembering the cliffs as he
ad seen them from the decks of the *Blackball Annie*. Mat
aid if he could climb twenty feet he would be all right.
Harold knew that was a lie. He had estimated the cliffs
ere a hundred and fifty feet at least. Seen from the trawler
hey had looked sheer, and almost completely devoid of
egetation.

"Well, what about it?" Mat demanded. "We can't stop
ere chewin' the cud all night. Tide's on the turn, and in
n hour or so there won't be nothing to stand on."

"Nobody could climb these cliffs in darkness," Harold
rotested. "I've done rock-climbing, and I know."

Mat was silent for a moment, then he said soberly.

"There's five of us here, Mr. Jackson. I might be able
o climb high enough to keep from being drowned. You
ight. But these Frenches won't climb. They can't. They'd
e stuck on that reef for hours before we got to 'em. They're
xhausted. Two of 'em are hurt. See what I mean. I can't
in for help. I've got a dicky ankle. Now . . . that leaves
nly you." He held up a hand, three fingers upright, though
arold could not see them in the darkness. "Three men
epending on you. You say you can't climb . . . h'm! That
eans three dead Frenchmen. Pity, after all they've gone
hrough, eh? Pity. I'll bet they've got wives an' families,
o."

Harold gulped, then asked in a husky voice:

"What do I do when I get to the top?"

"Turn right, when you gets to the top," Mat said slowly,

"and there's a lighthouse about nine miles down the coast.

"Nine miles!" Harold was aghast at the news. He wa
certain he would never be able to walk nine miles.

"Let me finish," Mat said calmly. "There'll be someor
on their way here at this very minute. The lighthous
keeper would pick up the *Jean's* S O S and I daresay there
a rescue party almost here at this minute. You keep you
eyes skinned for sight of a lantern. Guide the party here
He patted Harold on the shoulder, and there was somethin
almost like a chuckle in his voice as he added: "By the tin
I've finished with you, m'lad, even old Josh wouldn't kno
you. I'll make a man out of you. Aye, mebbe as good a ma
as your grandfather was, and that's saying something, fo
they didn't make 'em better than Josh no time. Now, o
you go, an' good luck!" To himself, as Harold moved t
the cliff face, Mat murmured: "And you'll need the luc!
every bit there is going, so you will."

Harold scarcely felt the pain of his bare feet as he move
along the shingle, feeling for handholds to start the clim
up the cliff. He was cold, shivering, and afraid. Wheneve
he had done rock-climbing before, there had been rope
and a guide. It had been broad daylight. Now . . . it wa
dark, and he was to climb alone.

Feeling for the first finger-holds. Harold began to clim
Had it not been pitch black, he would never have starte
for the apparently unclimbable face of the cliff would hav
daunted him. As it was, finding a finger-hold, he levere
himself off the shingle, and, finding his bare feet grippe
much better than any climbing boots he had ever wor
he began to work his way up.

His fingers were sore, and his toes were soon skinned, bu
the sheer effort of climbing overshadowed everything els

Once he was a few feet up, he knew he would not be able to return. Climbing down a cliff face was worse than going up.

Time after time he had to stop and rest, and as he hugged the rock he could feel its faint trembling. Mighty waves were smashing to foam along the length of the coast, thundering in at some points right to the cliff itself. The thought that the tide was on the turn, and that very soon the little strip of shingle would be under water kept him going. Mat Webber's words rang through his head like a warning bell . . . "You say you can't climb. Hm! Pity. That means three dead Frenchmen." It meant more than that. It would mean a dead Mat Webber, and that was something Harold refused to contemplate. Mat Webber he had looked upon as a bully, a blue-nosed mate of the old school. The kind of man who got obedience by means of a marlin-spike, or knuckle-dusters. Well, Harold had changed his views. As he saw Mat now, he was a hero. A man who never gave up. A man who did not seem to know what pain or fatigue meant.

It was this which kept Harold going when his arm muscles were like lead and his toes were raw and bleeding.

How long he had been climbing before he saw the glimmer of a light, he did not know. It might have been an hour; it might have been several hours. He had lost all sense of time, all feeling. His hands and legs moved automatically, feeling for tiny crevices, the merest indentation of rock which would give him a finger- or toe-hold.

Then, out of the corner of his eye, he saw the light. For a moment or so he stopped climbing, and stared. He was too benumbed to realise immediately that the thing he was seeing, a yellow blob in the darkness, waving about, must be a lantern, and must mean another human being.

Then, before he had quite decided the light was not a tric
of his fevered imagination, he saw another light. Thi
time it was a white light . . . like a shooting star, but muc
more vivid and brilliant. This light curved up out of th
darkness in a growing aura of brilliant whiteness. Then i
seemed to explode, and at once began to drop slowly dow
towards the sea.

It was a magnesium flare, familiar enough during th
Hitler war, for it was used by pilots to see what lay belo
them. Now it was showing the angry tossing of the sea
the black-fanged rocks, and the glistening face of the blac
cliffs. It showed something else, too . . . the bows of th
unhappy *Jean*. Very soon after Mat, Harold, and the Frenc
man had left the trawler, the broken bows had been swep
off the ledge of rock and, caught in a tidal race, had bee
swept to the east for two or three hundred yards befor
coming to rest once more on another rocky ledge.

The rescue team were now trying to get a response fror
the battered forepeak of the *Jean*, hoping that if there wer
survivors still clinging to that pathetic fragment of th
trawler they would show a signal of some kind.

Forgetting that his voice was but a mere piping in th
roar of the seas and the drone of the wind, Harold bega
to shout.

"Here . . . here. This way! Come this way!" He shoute
until his voice died away into a husky whisper. Then h
waited, hoping to see that yellow blob of light begin t
come nearer. Instead, another magnesium flare was fire
upwards, and dropping seawards cast a ghastly white ligh
over the sea and the bows of the *Jean*. It was obvious ther
even to the dazed Harold, that the rescue team had no
heard him.

"Why don't they see me?" he whispered. "Why don't they look this way?" It seemed as if anyone with eyes must see him perched there on the gaunt, bare rock face. The brilliance of the flares lit up everything for a couple of hundred yards or more, and threw into vivid details the battered portion of the wrecked trawler.

The flare drifted lower and lower, burned to a red pinpoint, and was suddenly extinguished as it fell into the water.

Wearily, Harold began to climb again. He felt it was useless. If these men were so blind as not to see him, they would probably soon go away . . . long before he could climb to the cliff top.

Then, quite unexpectedly, he reached for a hand-hold, and there was nothing there. The cliff seemed to have vanished. He pawed the air, his legs suddenly beginning to tremble. In desperation he heaved himself higher, leaned forward, and fell gently on to the cliff top. When he first saw the rescue-teams' light, he had been within ten feet of the top, and had not known it.

For five minutes he lay there, with the rain beating down on him. The reaction of reaching the top, when somehow he had never imagined he would do the trick, left him limp. It was as if his steel-taut nerves had suddenly given up the ghost.

The cliff top was unlike cliff tops in Britain. It was devoid of vegetation of any kind. No springy turf, just hard, cold, wet earth; yet it felt comfortable. The exhaustion of his reserve powers left him in a semi-drugged state. Cold, hunger, terror, he felt none of them. All he was aware of was that he had reached the top of the cliff; he was safe; and he was lying down. He need only close his eyes and he could sink into a deep and wonderful sleep.

He moved himself to get a more comfortable position, and might have closed his eyes again had he not caught a glimpse for a second of that irritating yellow blob of light. It was moving again, perhaps three hundred yards away on the cliff top. Then he suddenly knew he could not stay there. The light was growing smaller. The rescue team had given up the search. They must be going back to the lighthouse.

Harold got to his feet, and the Goddess of Good Fortune must have had her hands on his shoulders that night. He might easily have stumbled over the cliff in the darkness, for he was going forward in a shambling, uncertain run, weaving to this side and that as he now and then stubbed his bare feet on mounds, or put them in unexpected hollows.

It took twenty minutes of desperate running, falling, and running again before he finally caught up with the men carrying the lantern. There were two of them, and they were carrying bulky kits, and a heavy iron tripod, part of a rocket-firing apparatus. They were from the lighthouse, having received a wireless appeal, together with directions as to where the wrecked *Jean* was lying.

The men, unable to understand a word of English, helped Harold back to the spot where he estimated he had climbed the cliff. Then they went back for their equipment, after giving Harold a stiff tot of rum which chased some of the bitter cold from his body and shivering limbs.

They came staggering back with their gear, and how they had got that equipment over nine miles of trackless coastline only they knew.

Firing a flare down towards the strip of shingle, the men then lowered a long rope, to the free end of which they had secured a small lantern, its glass guarded by a wire frame.

Harold sat and watched, an oilskin about his wet body to keep off the cold wind.

The rope was paid out and out, until finally it went slack. One man shook the rope violently, just in case the lantern had got caught on a ledge; but the rope was still slack, proving that it had reached the shingle beach.

For a minute or so they waited. Harold was wondering if Mat Webber was busy tying one of the Frenchmen on the end of the rope. He waited for the jerk which would tell his would-be rescuers they could begin hauling . . . but the rope remained slack.

Finally the two Icelanders began hauling in the rope, while Harold watched their faces anxiously, wondering what they were thinking. At length the strong little lantern came into sight. It was as it had been when sent down . . . there was no message attached. Nothing to show that there was any living human below.

"Perhaps it isn't the right place," Harold stammered, but neither of the Icelanders understood a word he said. By signs, after a minute or so, they managed to convey to him the news that this was the only spot along the coast where anyone could land. Apart from that small strip of shingle beach on which Mat and the other four had landed, there was not another piece of beach for several miles.

The inference was obvious. Some time, while Harold had been climbing the cliff, or while he had been stumbling towards the rescue team, something had happened down at sea level. An extra large wave had washed in, sucked the four survivors off the shingle into the sea and drowned them. Or, alternatively, the tide had come up. If that had happened, there was no way out, no retreat, save up the cliff face.

"I'll go down," Harold said, getting to his feet and trying

to secure the long rope about his waist. "They must be down there. They must."

The two Icelanders shook a grave denial. To go down was out of the question, and a waste of time. Harold began to fumble again with the rope, but the rope was taken from him, gently but firmly. He tried to resist, but he was too weak.

Leaving their rescue apparatus to be carried back some other time, the two men began to half-walk, half-carry, Harold along the cliff top. They were sure there was no other survivor of the wreck, and they wanted to get this shivering youth to a place where new life could be given him . . . a warm bed, hot drinks, bandages for his hands and feet.

They had gone perhaps twenty yards, when, some dozen yards from the spot where the rescue kit lay, a dark figure heaved itself wearily over the cliff edge, and sprawled forward on the wet earth. It was Mat Webber.

Mat had decided he must make an effort to scale the cliff, in case Harold failed. Now, too exhausted to do anything, he lay there and watched the bobbing lantern moving farther and farther away. By its yellow light, he could see the two men and Harold between them.

There were limits to even Mat Webber's strength and endurance. He tried to get to his feet, but though the will was there, the strength had momentarily gone. Even his voice, of which he was so proud, was little more than a hoarse whisper when he called. It was a sound which the wind picked up and wafted away.

The bobbing lantern, the three figures, moved steadily away towards the nine-miles-distant lighthouse.

CHAPTER FOURTEEN

CHIP OFF THE OLD BLOCK

FOR PERHAPS three minutes, while they covered sixty or seventy yards of rough ground, Harold made no protest. Now that he had tried, and been forcibly prevented from attempting a cliff rescue, he was glad to be done with it all. Glad to be going towards safety, comfort, to be finished with the sea and all its terrors and pains. Then, into that cosy picture came another, the stern, rugged face of Mat Webber, and the mate's harsh voice seemed to ring again in Harold's ears. They were accusing words; the same words which had spurred him on to make his desperate cliff ascent:

"That means three dead Frenchmen. Pity, after all they've gone through."

Three dead Frenchmen and a dead Britisher. What was it Mat had said earlier: "If I don't get back, say 'Good-bye' to my missus." Then Mat had winked.

Without a word, Harold suddenly wrenched himself free from the grip of the two Icelanders. He turned on his heels and began to run back, ignoring the angry shouts of the two men. They were so taken aback that it was a few moments before they turned in pursuit.

Harold was young, and young people recover quickly from exhaustion. He ran well, and did not stop until he fell over Mat Webber, who was still trying to get to his feet. When the two men from the lighthouse arrived, their lantern guttering, they gaped at the sight of two people where they had expected to see only one.

"So you . . . made it?" Mat was croaking. "Well, I'm hanged. You'd only been gone a minute or two when I decided I'd been a fool to send you. Summat seemed to tell me you'd never do it. That's when I started to climb. You must have been a bit quicker than me."

"We thought you were drowned," Harold gasped. "Oh I'm glad . . . I'm glad. They lowered a lantern, but nobody seemed to have touched it. We were sure . . . well, they were, that the sea must have got you."

"Aye, I saw the lantern," Mat agreed, "but . . . I didn't have breath for shouting. Not built for climbin' cliffs . . . not at my age, anyway."

"I can't tell you how glad I am and . . . "

"Aye, well, shut up for a minute," Mat ordered. "This isn't the time for flag-waggin'. The tide's coming up, and there's three of 'em still down there; down and out they are. If they're to be saved, somebody'll have to go down for 'em."

By signs they managed to tell the two lighthouse men that there were still three people at the foot of the cliffs and that speed was essential if they were to be saved.

More pantomime acting by the light-house men made Harold and Mat realise that if anyone went down the cliff, it would have to be one of them. To haul anyone up the cliff needed strength, a strength neither Harold nor Mat possessed. What was more, the hands of both Britishers were so lacerated that to haul on a rope would be sheer agony.

Harold picked up the rope, and the end was knotted securely about his waist. Then, with a lantern in his right hand, he was lowered over the cliff. It was a nightmare journey, for he had to fend himself off the rock face for most of the time. At length, however, he was down to the shingle again.

The scene by the light of the lantern was frightening. The three Frenchmen were seated with their backs to the cliff, but now the water was higher, lapping about them, for the tide had turned and was coming in.

Harold managed to get the French skipper into the loops of the bo'sun's chair tied ready in the rope, then gave a jerk. The man was hauled up in a series of long quick hauls. The men up above knew the necessity of speed. Even so it was ten minutes before the rope came down again for the second man, and the tide was coming in fast.

He got the second man into the rope loops, and once again the men above got to work smoothly and quickly. Ten minutes and the rope was back once more; but this time, Harold was sweating in nervous fear. The shingle was completely covered, and with the undertow as each wave slid back, more and more shingle was pulled down. It was slipping from under his feet, and, when he did tug on the rope as a signal for the men up above to haul, he slipped and went floundering face down in water.

The shingle was very loose now, and a breaking wave curled over him as he was trying to get to his feet. It knocked him sideways, and he swallowed water before he recovered. Almost crying with vexation and fear, he fought his way up the moving shingle to the foot of the cliff.

It was then that the sea, with malicious cruelty, seemed to make a last desperate effort to claim one victim. A larger than usual wave splashed in, sucked the shingle from the bank, and Harold lost his balance once more. This time, however, in an attempt to keep his feet, he turned seawards, but the shingle moved from under him. He fell backwards, cracked his head against the rock wall, and collapsed in a sitting position, the water up to his armpits.

He was dazed; dazed and weary. He struggled a little but that only made the shingle move from under him, and the next wave broke over his face, making him gasp and choke. Vainly he fought to get to his feet, but his strength had gone.

He rolled sideways, tried to recover himself, but the shingle moved again, and the yellow gleam of the lantern propped on a ledge out of reach of the sea, threw a pale glimmer over him as he went beneath the surface.

It was then that a great heavy body hurtled down out of the night, knocking the lantern off its ledge and plunging it into the sea, where it went out at once.

Mat Webber sent water flying as he alighted on the shingle. His two powerful hands went out, clutched Harold just as the undertow was taking him down the disintegrating shingle bank, and dragged him clear. Mat gave a mighty jerk on the rope, and the two lighthousemen on top began what was to be a long, slow haul.

The last Frenchman up had said that Harold looked about all in, a piece of news which had made Mat decide to go down. It was a move which saved the last of the Jacksons. Another minute and the sea would have claimed a victim.

It took twenty-four hours to get the rescued men to the nine-miles-distant lighthouse, but there a fresh rescue squad took over. The Frenchmen were taken to Reykjavik for hospital treatment. The two Britishers stayed at the lighthouse. All they needed, apart from sundry pieces of plaster, and one or two bandages about skinned knees and hands, was rest.

Three days later, Harold Jackson went with Mat Webber to a cove four miles from the lighthouse. Two trawlers were standing a mile off shore. They had their trawls neatly stowed, for to be caught within the three-mile limit with gear ready for fishing can mean arrest and a fine of up to £1,000.

One trawler was the *Blackball Annie*, the other the *Toros*. The *Toros* had been called in by Mike Grory because the small boat of the *Annie* had been smashed up. Deckhands of the *Toros* pulled inshore and took aboard the mate and the owner of the *Annie*.

"Well, it won't be long before you're home now," Mat said, as they settled themselves in the stern of the small boat. "The *Toros* is about two knots faster than the *Annie*. I daresay at a pinch he could get twelve knots."

Harold looked at the mate of the *Annie*. Mat carried plenty of evidence of the ordeal he had gone through. His hands were bandaged. One side of his face was badly bruised, and he had a black eye. Harold's hands were also in bandages, while his feet were encased in large-size carpet-slippers to give room for the cotton wool and bandages there. His face was puffed, and there was a healing patch on one cheek where the skin had been scraped badly during his descent of the cliff.

"We'll go to the *Annie* first," he said soberly. "I've some scores to settle before I go home."

"Oh?" Mat Webber cocked an interrogative eyebrow, but made no other comment. He had rather imagined that Harold Jackson, new owner of the Jackson Trawlers, would have forgotten, or forgiven, all that had taken place aboard the *Annie* prior to the wreck of the *Jean*.

The sea was very calm, and the two trawlers were standing

about a cable's length apart, the merest wisp of smoke rising
from the tall funnels. Deckhands lined the rails, and once
the small boat was within easy hailing distance, there were
yells and cheers of acclamation. Mat's name came over the
water, loud and clear. Harold was not mentioned by name,
for word had got round that he was old Josh Jackson's
grandson, new owner of the trawling fleet, and most of the
men were wondering what was going to happen. The men
of the *Toros* had heard that Harold had been given the rough
end of things, and so everyone was curious to see what
would happen now.

There had been plenty of discussions about Harold during
the past three days. The general opinion was that there
couldn't be much wrong with a bloke who would risk his
life to take a line over to a wrecked trawler as Harold had
done; on the other hand, the new owner had shown himself
to be a bit of a Tartar.

There was a strange silence as the boat was pulled alongside the *Annie*. The crew were lining the rail, smoking and
watching. Mike Grory was there, and it was he who helped
Harold over the rail. Mat, despite his bandaged hands,
refused any help.

Harold turned to the crew of the small boat.

"Give the captain of the *Toros* my compliments and
thanks," he said gravely, "and tell him to proceed with
his fishing."

The boat was pushed away, the oars dipped, and the men
were silent until they were almost under the stern of their
own craft, then the mate of the *Toros* gave a long, low
whistle.

"If that's the new boss, lads," he said grimly, "I can see
there'll be a lot of changes pretty soon. I shan't fancy

working under him. The cold-blooded little devil. You'd have thought he'd have treated us all to a drop of tiddly to celebrate, wouldn't you?"

On the *Blackball Annie* there were a few moments of awkward silence. Then Mike Grory held out his right hand, a smile of welcome on his face.

"I want to say right away, Mr. Jackson, that you are a chip off the old block, and no mistake about it. I wasn't able to see you take that line over to the *Jean*, but I'll tell you this, they're talking about it on all the ships up Iceland way, and I'll bet it's been in all the papers back home."

"Before we start patting one another on the back," Harold said gravely, "I think we'd better have a little chat. Will you come along to the chartroom, Mr. Webber. I have something to say to you, as well."

The deckhands were silent as statues. They had been ready, and anxious, to applaud this youth for the courage he had shown; but there was something in the air which suggested cheers might be out of place. There was a grimness about Harold Jackson's mouth the men did not like.

Harold stood aside while Mike Grory led the way into the chartroom, Mat followed, and Harold came last.

"This," said Harold, "is what we might call ' settling day'. I think I promised earlier on in the trip that my turn would come."

"I seem to remember something of the sort," Mike admitted gravely. "Go on, Mr. Jackson, I'm listening."

"I tried to explain to you that I was Harold Jackson, but you laughed at me. Well . . . there is a saying that ' He who laughs last laughs best.'"

"I have heard of that saying," Mike admitted.

"I'll tell you something else," Harold went on. "One o
the many things my grandfather taught me was never t
make a promise unless I intended to keep it."

"A very commendable thing," Mike said, nodding again

"I promised I would fire you both, didn't I?" Harold said
"And I always try to keep my promises, so . . ."

"Here, wait a minute," it was Mat Webber, and there wa
fire in his eyes. "Now, listen to me. If anybody had tol
me an hour back that you'd do this, I'd have knocked thei
block off, yes, and enjoyed doing it. I wouldn't have believe
it for a thousand quid. You've got guts, I've seen enoug
to know that; but you ain't got what it takes to make
good man. You ain't got an ounce of charity in you. Yo
aren't fit to own a wash tub, let alone a fleet of trawlers
And if you think you're going to fire me, you're mistook
I resign. You can take it from this very minute."

"Thank you, that's just what I wanted," Harold sai
coolly, and turning to Mike he said evenly. "Now, Mr
Grory, I'll be kind to you. Would you like to resign a
skipper of the *Annie*, or shall I discharge you?"

"You'll have to fire me," Mike said curtly. "But, befor
you do anything like that, I'm going to ask you one im
portant question. Who do you think is going to take th
Annie back to port?"

"Mr. Webber will do that," The reply came out pat. "I an
appointing him skipper of the *Blackball Annie* from thi
moment."

"You know what you can do with that job," was Mat'
prompt retort.

"Quite," Harold refused to be ruffled. "I am giving yo
command of the *Annie*. I am giving Mr. Grory comman
of our latest trawler. She should be ready for sea in a few

weeks' time. I remember my grandfather talking to me about her. She's a five-hundred tonner, diesel-engined, and will show a clean pair of heels to any trawler in the world. At least, that was what my grandfather said, when he told me he meant to give the new boat to his best skipper . . Mr. Mike Grory."

For once Harold had both Mike and Mat completely nonplussed. They simply stood and stared.

Harold went on:

"I don't know whether Grandfather had a name for the new trawler; but I've been thinking about it. I'd like it to be known as the *Josh Jackson*. What do you think of that?"

Mike shook his head.

"Well . . . it isn't often I have my leg pulled, Mr. Jackson," he said, and now the tightness of his mouth had changed to a smile. "But you've put one over on me and Mat very nicely."

"I said I'd fire you both . . . and, I've done it," Harold said, and chuckled. "There's just one other thing. I want you to accept my very sincere apologies for the trouble I caused you. When I came aboard I was what the fellows at my school would call a real ' stinker ' ."

Mike Grory chuckled, nodded, then said:

"Your grandfather asked me to see that some of your conceit was knocked out of you. We did our best."

Harold grinned.

"I can appreciate the joke now," he said, "but I hated you both earlier on. I wouldn't have believed that I could learn so much in such a short time."

"If you keep learnin' as fast as you have done, Mr. Jackson," Mat Webber said earnestly, "it won't be long before

your name will be as respected as your grandfather's was,
and is. If you know what I mean."

Harold flushed. From Mat Webber that was praise indeed.

"Thank you, and I'd rather you dropped the ' Mister ', if
you don't mind. To my friends, I am Harold. I hope I can
call you both friend, now."

Mike Grory thrust out his hand.

"Harold," he said quietly. "I knew your father, just
slightly. He would have been a great man if the war hadn't
taken him. Well, I think you'll do what he might have
done if he'd lived. You'll step right into old Josh's shoes . . .
and they won't pinch at the toes."

Harold had nothing to say for a moment. There was a
lump in his throat. Then he forced a laugh.

"Listen, gentlemen, I don't drink, but I think there ought
to be some celebration. You two have been promoted, and
I am hoping to step out of the shoes of a silly, conceited
youth and become a man willing to learn more about
trawling. I wonder if the crew of this trawler, and of the
Toros, would like to drink our health? I suppose we have
some whisky or rum aboard."

"We have both," Mike assured him, "and I think maybe
the deckhands would toast us. You can ask them." And
there was a twinkle in his eyes as he said that.

Mike brought whisky from the ship's bond, and the crew
collected mugs from the cook's galley. While they were
being served with their tot, Harold was collecting his
clothing from the chartroom. There was a bedraggled
sports jacket, a blue silk sports shirt, a stained and oil-
smeared pair of flannels, two shoes which were hardly
worth putting on a ragman's cart, and a canary yellow
pull-over.

He stood on the top of the ladder for a moment, while the deckhands on the foredeck held up their mugs to him, to Mike and to Mat.

"There's one thing I'd like you to forget . . . for the rest of the trip, if you can," he said. "Forget that I am the new owner of the Jackson Trawlers. I was put aboard to have some of the corners knocked off me. That's why I'm moving my things back to the fo'c'sle. I'm going to finish the trip as I began, apprentice stoker. I hope you won't mind."

Mugs were held up, drained, and then the deckhands of the *Blackball Annie* gave him a rousing cheer.

In the wheelhouse, Mat Webber licked his lips, looked regretfully at his empty mug, then said:

"If old Josh had been livin' to-day, Mike, there wouldn't have been a prouder man breathin'. That kid's a chip off the old block, and no two ways about it."

"And I'll bet he's the last person ever to be shanghaied aboard a trawler," Mike said. Then: "Well, we're wasting time. I want a few more hauls before I turn for home."

"Here, that'll do my lad," Mat said, and with a grin reminded him: "You're forgetting something, aren't you? I'm the new skipper. You be nice to me or I'll throw you off, neck and crop."

For a moment, even Mike looked startled. Then he grinned. Yes, he had forgotten that. He was only a passenger, but there was a five-hundred-ton trawler waiting for him when he got back to port. And he would be working under a new boss, a young boss, but a boss he felt he was going to like. Harold Jackson had proved himself in the past few days.

"Shoot-oh," Mat yelled, leaning out of the wheelhouse window. "Come on, you lazy scabs, get that trawl down

where the *sprags* are. I'm going to show you, and the cod
that there's somebody aboard the *Annie* what knows how to
fish. From now on, you'll really work for your living."
His voice was harsh enough, but there was a twinkle in his
eyes, and the crew gave him the Icelandic "Yes" in a deep
voiced chorus of: "YOW" before scattering to shoot the
trawl.

THE END